IN THE SHADOW
OF DEATH

By Walter B. Littlejohn, Jr.

ISBN: 1-4392-0045-9
ISBN-13: 9781439200452

Visit www.booksurge.com to order additional copies.

PART ONE

THE WAR YEARS

1941

Lead, kindly Light, amid the encircling gloom,

Lead thou me on!

The night is dark, and I am far from home-

Lead thou me on!

Keep thou my feet; I do not ask to see

The distant scene, one step enough for me.

– The Pillar of the Cloud. by John Henry Newman

CHAPTER 1

The latest weapon of The United States Submarine Service, The USS Mackerel, like some giant ocean predator, slides silently below the surface of the South China Sea on its maiden voyage. Its skipper, Lt. Commander William D. Richardson, scanned the surface of the water through the periscope, looking for the ship he and his crew had been stalking for the last eight hours. The sonar operator had detected the sound of a slow-moving freighter shortly before 11 p.m., but it was a dark, moonless night, and since Richardson hadn't been able to see the blacked-out ship, he'd played the waiting game. Trailing the target throughout the night, maintaining sonar contact until daylight, when, hopefully, a visual sighting could be made.

The Mackerel was one of four subs that had been sent to the South China Sea to prey on any type of Japanese ship they could find. So far, it had been a highly successful sortie. Each sub in the pack had a designated area to patrol, with The Mackerel lucky enough to be assigned to an area heavily traveled by all manner of Japanese ships. During the three weeks the Mackerel had cruised the area, it had made four kills on freighters and tankers and had heavily damaged a Japanese cruiser before being driven off by a speedy Japanese destroyer. Richardson had pulled every trick he knew to dodge the depth charges, zigzagging and changing depth, but explosions had come so close at times that the concussion knocked crewmen off their feet and caused the lights to flicker. To escape the relentless pursuit, he dived deep into the murky waters, shut down the engines and drifted silently as the destroyer prowled back and forth above them.

But now there was no destroyer to hunt them down and hitting the slow-moving freighter would be like shooting fish in a barrel. It would be a good kill. If it were a freighter, there would be just so much less ammo or supplies for the Japs to use. If it were a troop ship, he could kill, literally in minutes, more enemy soldiers than a whole regiment of infantry in a dozen battles. He raised the periscope at the exact time he knew the sun would rise out of the ocean. As he pivoted the scope to the west, he saw it. It would come briefly into view and then disappear again in the heavy seas, but now he knew exactly where it was. As he maneuvered into position for attack, he kept it in constant view. It was an old ship, its hull covered in a patchwork of rust and belching a thick column of black smoke from its funnel.

Richardson watched the ship for several minutes and then with four words, he sealed the fate of the Japanese ship.

"Fire one," and then "Fire two."

Watching through the periscope, his heart raced as he followed the torpedo wakes streaking toward the ship. It was always this way. The war had been going on for three years and every time he launched a torpedo, he always got that same rush of adrenaline. Then a plume of water, followed by another as the torpedoes slammed into the lumbering ship. Within minutes, the ship rolled on it's side and slipped beneath the waves.

As a career military officer, Richardson had been trained to kill, but like most warriors, he had been taught that when an enemy could no longer do you harm, you did him no further harm. It was his practice, when possible, to rescue any survivors of his deadly attacks. Making certain once again that there were no Japanese warships nearby, he ordered The Mackerel to surface. As soon as the conning tower was clear of the surface he scrambled up the ladder. As he emerged from the hatch the acrid smell of burning oil filled his nostrils. The water was ablaze with a quickly spreading oil slick and there was very little debris to show that a ship had ever existed. As he scanned the area through his binoculars he could see heads being engulfed by flames...there was nothing he could do to save them. Suddenly one of the crewmen shouted,

"There's one over there."

Turning in the direction the sailor was pointing, he trained his binoculars on what appeared to be a hunk of wood floating clear of the blazing oil. At first, that was all he could see, a piece of floating wood, but when it rose on an ocean swell, he saw the man draped unconscious across the flotsam.

Racing the spreading flames, a dinghy was launched and the unconscious man was plucked from the sea and brought aboard The Mackerel.

Later, as medic's cleaned the oil and grime from the man's face, his eyes blinked and then opened. When he raised his arm to shield his eyes from the bright overhead light, Doc Lewis, the boats surgeon, saw an American Eagle tattoo on the left shoulder.

"Go get the skipper. This is no Jap."

CHAPTER 2

In January 1941, Jack joined the army straight out of high school. It had been a difficult decision. Jack was madly in love with Laura. They had been "going steady" since their sophomore year in high school. He, the star athlete and she, the pert blond cheerleader. Together they were the most popular couple to walk hand in hand down the halls of North Dallas High.

Jack never doubted that Laura would someday be his wife and the mother of his children. But with the war already raging in Europe he was sure to be drafted if he didn't enlist. He considered a year or two in the Army just a slight detour in the normal course of his life. On their last night together, Jack put a nickel in the drive-ins jukebox and they sat staring into each other's eyes.

Gripping his hand, blue eyes glistening with tears, Laura said, "There'll never be anyone else but you and I promise I'll be here when you come home."

After basic training at Fort Sam Houston, he was assigned to the 201st Artillery Regiment at Fort Bliss. The raw recruits underwent intense training learning to use the 75-mm guns, which could be used as antiaircraft defense or as ground artillery. After two months of training in the New Mexico desert, they were ready to be sent overseas. Daily rumors circulated about where they would be sent. One day it would be England. The next day, North Africa. Finally, official word came that they would be sent to the Philippines. Most people in the United States didn't expect the country to get involved in the war that raged in Europe...what went on in Europe wasn't their problem and most didn't really care that Hitler's *Blitzkrieg* had already rolled across half of Europe. To the men of the 201st, the transfer of a combat-ready unit in the opposite direction was further proof that the United States wasn't going to get into an unpopular war.

The train from El Paso to San Francisco had taken six weary days, often sitting for hours on some railway siding waiting for another train to clear the tracks ahead. When they did move, the hot desert air blasted through the open windows of the swaying coach like a blowtorch and cinders from the engine covered everything with a fine layer of soot. Every seat was occupied by young soldiers, their khakis rumpled, forest green ties hanging loosely around their necks. They slept sitting up, the hot, coarse upholstery chafing the skin. Small groups huddled in the aisles shooting the bull while they passed around bottles of cheap whiskey. Others whiled away the miles with nonstop card games. As they entered the outskirts of San Francisco, talk turned to the fabled city's nightlife and how they would teach these California women a thing or two about real men.

But much to their dismay, they went straight through the city and stopped within sight of the docks, and as they stepped off the train, they were assembled and marched directly to a ship.

The ship Jack and the other members of the 201st boarded wasn't much to look at and despite a fresh coat of paint, it was obviously older than most of the men now going up the gangplank. In places the black paint on the hull appeared to have been unevenly applied over the top of previous coats. On the stern, in bright, new white letters, Jack could see the name, *USS Republic.*

The gangplank swayed and sagged under the men's weight as they hauled up their entire worldly possessions in olive drab duffel bags slung over one shoulder. Jack had learned, almost from the first day, that the army did everything within its power to strip you of your individuality so all the men boarding the troop ship, except for a few personal items like pictures and letters from home, had exactly the same items in their duffel bags. Six pairs of socks, six pair of underwear, six undershirts, a rubber poncho, one pair of black combat boots, and a nylon zip-up kit with razor, toothbrush and necessary toiletries. Their M-1's were slung over their other shoulder, and a canvas-covered canteen hung from a tan web belt around their waists.

The disappointment at not getting to see San Francisco was lessened by the excitement Jack felt as he boarded the ship. He had never been on a ship before. Now he was boarding a ship that would take him all the way across the Pacific Ocean to exotic places only dreamed of.

"Awright, awright get the lead out of your arses. We ain't got all day. Get below and find a place to bunk," the burly sergeant bellowed just as Jack passed him at the top of the gangplank. Jack turned his face away as the hot breath, reeking of whiskey, burst from the sergeant's mouth.

"Come on, Charlie. Let's get bunks together."

Charlie Jones and Jack had become friends at Fort Sam despite being as different as two people could be. Even though he had lost his beautiful head of black wavy hair within an hour of stepping off the bus at Fort Sam, Jack still had the good looks and outgoing personality that had won him the hearts of all the girls and the title of "Most Popular Boy" his senior year. A strapping six foot three inches and 210 pounds, Jack had had been the first four-sport letterman in the long history of North Dallas High School. Jack came by his good looks and athleticism naturally. His father, tall and outgoing just like Jack, had also been a star athlete in high school and his mother, a stunning redhead had been a model for the Neiman's store in Dallas before Michael Collins came into her life

Charlie, on the other hand, was short and stocky with muscular arms and slightly bowed legs. Dark, wide-set eyes peered out from under heavy brows and his nose looked like it had been broken numerous times. The son of a bronco rider on the rodeo circuit, he had spent most of his life moving through small southwestern towns in a beat-up Ford pickup with a camper on the back. He had never known his mother, and his father never spoke of her. Charlie started to ride broncos when he was 16 and got an ugly scar on the side of his left knee when a horse named *Wild Thing* reared up in the chute and pinned his leg against the fence. When he was 18, his father was kicked in the head by a bronco and died two days later in the small hospital in Lampassas, Texas.

Charlie drifted to San Antonio and when he saw a poster that said, *"UNCLE SAM WANTS YOU"* he went into the recruiting office and joined up. A loner, Charlie seemed unfriendly to most people and the first week in basic, Charlie-because-of his size and personality-was easy prey for the bullies in the unit. But Jack...at first from sympathy and later through genuine affection...became his protector; the taunts and practical jokes quickly ended. After that, Jack and Charlie were inseparable.

As the initial excitement of embarking on their great adventure wore off, days began to run together and Jack soon lost all track of how long they'd been at sea. Time had never been that important to him, and now that he was in the army, his time was totally under someone else's control. You were told when to get up, when to eat, when to go to drill, when to shine your shoes, and when to go to bed. Charlie had once joked, "The day they start telling me when to take a shit is the day I get out of this man's army."

Their day would start at 5:30 a.m. every morning except Sunday, when a non-com would stick his head through the hatch and bellow, "Drop your cocks and grab your socks, it's time to get up and at em." On Sundays they could sleep in, but if you wanted breakfast you had to be in the mess galley by 8 a.m.

On the trip to the Philippines, they had very little to do except make their bunks, police the area they lived in, clean their guns every day, and write letters to the folks back home. They were told that the salt air would ruin the guns and that a coat of oil every day was the only way to make sure they would have a weapon they could depend on. There would be work details to scrub the deck or KP in the galley cleaning pots and pans but, for the most part, it was hard to fight the boredom.

There was always a raucous crap game with a half dozen sweating, kneeling men, sleeves rolled up, cigarettes dangling from their mouths, rolling dice against a steel bulkhead. Shouts of "come on seven, baby needs a new pair of shoes" would reverberate from the steel plates. When a player won there would be whoops of delight while the losers would curse their bad luck. Non-stop poker games were scattered around the hold. The men would sit around metal footlockers, their heads enveloped in a haze of blue smoke and players would drop out only when they had lost all their money. Jack didn't gamble, but Charlie did. There had been a poker game every night on the rodeo circuit, and by the time he was 15, Charlie joined the men's games. When his father died he had $19 in his pocket. That $19 and the old pickup, was his inheritance…that and how to play a good hand of poker.

One day as Jack sat on his bunk writing to Laura, he sensed that something had changed. The throb of the engines had changed in intensity and he felt them moving at a slower speed. Looking up from the paper he could see other men pause and look around as they too felt the difference. Leaving his bunk, Jack made his way to the deck where to his left, he could see that they were moving slowly past an island and beyond the island was a lush green jungle separated from the blue sea by a narrow strip of white sand.

"That's Corregidor."

Startled, Jack turned to see the imposing figure of Master Sgt. Samuel Malloy. Even at 6'3" Jack had to look up at the man who had been the recruits greatest tormentor for the past six months. From the first day of basic when Malloy had told them they were nothing but a group of snotty nosed young punks, he had constantly berated them for the least deviation from his exacting standards. Thrusting his massive chest as close as he could without knocking a man backwards, he would bellow that the barracks weren't clean enough, the shoes and brass didn't have a high shine, or their ranks weren't perfectly aligned. Even the "shavetails" who had just earned their gold bars held him in awe and rarely countermanded Malloy's orders. But now, Malloy was standing at Jack's side and talking like they had been lifetime friends.

"I was at Corregidor on my last hitch here and let me tell you, it's a fortress. Concrete bunkers with walls six feet thick and guns that could blow this tub out of the water in five minutes. And they've got tunnels dug in the hills where you can hole up and hold out forever. Stockpiles of food, ammo and medicine that'll last for years. Look there, you can see some of the guns." Jack squinted and saw a flash of light as the sun reflected off metal.

"That land behind Corregidor is Bataan," said Malloy "and you can't see it yet, but up ahead there is Manila."

CHAPTER 3

Jack's regiment was loaded into large Army trucks bound for their new post. As yet, they had not been told which of the many installations scattered throughout the Philippines would be their assignment, and there was much excited talk and speculation as to how close they would be to Manila's bars and beautiful women.

His best friends...Charlie Jones, Dick Gaddis, Bobby Hartsell, Buster Bowles, and Enos Hatfield...had all gotten on the same truck. On the ride from the ship, the trucks passed through Manila's tenderloin district known for its bars and prostitutes. They stared at the gaudy neon signs and girls...girls everywhere...some very pretty. Some were walking arm in arm with sailors or Army GI's, while others clustered on corners waving to them as they passed. Jack had never seen anything like it. At one point, while they were stopped in traffic, a young boy ran up behind the truck and yelled, "Hey GI, you want to fuck my mother? She's a virgin."

Enos, a slow talking, redheaded, freckled face boy from Georgia, brought laughter from everyone when he said, "Now, I don't believe that for one josh durn minute."

Just past the outskirts of Manila the trucks turned off the main road and passed under a large white sign …Fort William McKinley, P.I. They had arrived at their new home.

* * *

3,000 kilometers to the north, Lt. Kenji Tanaka sat in the small ornamental garden of his parents' house in the Asukusa district of Tokyo, eagerly awaiting the arrival of his good friend, Takeo Kamura. The garden was Kenji's favorite place. A footbridge arched over a small pond filled with carp and his father had artfully decorated the space with stone lanterns and dwarf Juniper.

Takeo had been his best friend since childhood, and they had taken different paths only when Kenji decided on a career in the army and Takeo became a naval aviator. Now, they were on leave at the same time and could spend a few hours reminiscing. There was great rivalry between the Army and Navy and their respective leaders were often at odds as to which course Japan should take in its fight for dominance in Southeast Asia. Both sides agreed on one thing...Japan was being slowly strangled by the United States oil embargo; to survive Japan had to gain control of the oil rich territories of the Dutch East Indies. Germany's recent victories in Europe convinced many that now was the perfect time to strike. Army leaders believed this could best be done by ground operations into Indochina. If the United States intervened with their Pacific Fleet they would be drawn into waters far from home, and with supply lines stretched dangerously thin, could easily be defeated by the Imperial Navy. Naval leaders, on the other hand, believed that success depended on the destruction of the Pacific Fleet while it sat at anchor in Pearl Harbor.

Kenji heard Takeo's voice as he was greeted by his father and waited for him to be ushered to the garden. After an exchange of formal bows, Kenji embraced his old friend.

"Takeo, How are you?"

"I'm good Kenji and I see army life is agreeing with you.."

"Stand back. Let me see you in your uniform." Kenji, much taller than Takeo held him at arm's length. "I'll bet you're the best pilot in the navy. Come sit down and tell me all about yourself." Kenji led Takeo to a bench at one side of the garden.

"Well, let's see. I'm now assigned to the *Akagi* and I consider it an honor because, as you may know, the *Akagi* is the flagship of the 1st Air Fleet. I see Admiral Nagumo nearly every day," said Takeo.

"Takeo, I envy you, soaring through the sky like a bird while I get blisters on my feet trudging down some dusty road."

Takeo laughed. "Well there's the matter of landing on a carrier deck that's bouncing around like a cork in the ocean. And sometimes at night no less. It scares me every time I do it."

"I've never seen you afraid of anything," Kenji slapped Takeo on the back.

Kenji leaned closer so that his father could not hear from the next room. "Tell me what you hear about our plans for dealing with the Americans. Everyone I know believes that we must do something."

"Everyone in the Navy believes this too. Do you know that we only have about four months' supply of oil to operate the fleet? After that, we won't be able to move a ship out of the harbor."

"I didn't know it was that bad."

Takeo leaned closer and spoke in a near whisper. "Yes, and I will tell you something else. The war games at the Naval War College simulated a war against the United States, with an attack against their fleet at Pearl Harbor and simultaneous attacks throughout the Pacific."

"But Takeo, this is only September. The war games are always held in December."

"To move them ahead three months shows how serious the situation is."

"What do you believe will happen?"

Takeo said, "I believe we'll be at war before the end of the year."

Kenji Tanaka grew up in Tokyo, the only son of a minor bank official and his young wife. His great-grandfather was an American seaman who met his great-grandmother in a Yokohama bar. Before the American returned to sea a week later, she was pregnant with his grandfather. Dishonored, his great-grandmother was permanently cast out of the family as if infected with a deadly plague. The American seaman never returned, and his great-grandmother died giving birth to his grandfather Tanaka. As much as the family wanted to hide the fact, there was no denying that American blood ran through the veins of his grandfather's descendents. Kenji had grown to over six feet and had the round eyes of a westerner.

Like most young men of his time, Kenji was groomed to be a member of the Imperial Army. Almost continual war in Korea, China and Russia during the past forty years had created a great demand for soldiers. Now early in 1941, Kenji had completed formal training at the *Ichigaya* Military Academy and had been commissioned a Lieutenant in the Imperial Army. Studies of everything from military doctrine to foreign languages, strenuous physical conditioning, almost total isolation from their families, and Spartan living conditions were designed to mold the young Japanese men into the world's deadliest fighters.

Kenji strove to be the best cadet to ever go through the Academy and felt he was ready to take his place among the officers of the Imperial Army. To be anything less would not only be a personal disappointment but would bring dishonor to himself and his family. From the beginning, they had been told they were superior to all other races. The underlying theme throughout their training had been to foster an undying loyalty and patriotism, blind obedience to orders, and a character that would never accept defeat.

CHAPTER 4

Capt. Robert E. Lee Clark, United States Military Academy, Class of '31, was the son of a staunch southerner who believed that the leader of the Confederate army was the greatest man that ever lived. At West Point, he had studied the tactics and war plans of the world's major conflicts. When they studied the Civil War, it was easy to see why his father held Robert E. Lee in such high esteem. A southern gentleman who reluctantly joined the rebel cause, Lee had, through his "offensive-defensive" strategy, almost pulled off the greatest upset in the history of warfare.

Now as he sat at his desk in A Battery headquarters at Fort William McKinley, a document with **"SECRET"** stamped across its face lay open on the gray metal desk. The document was the War Plan from General MacArthur's headquarters. After reading it, he wondered if the American forces in the Philippines were going to be used as the proverbial sacrificial lamb. The plan, known as "Plan Orange," outlined strategy in the event of an enemy invasion and called for token resistance at the landing beaches, then a delaying action while withdrawing all forces into the Bataan Peninsula where a six-month stand would be made until reinforcements could arrive. General MacArthur believed that if he could consolidate the American and Filipino forces in Bataan, he could establish a defensive line across the 20-mile width of the peninsula where it jutted into the South China Sea and, with the big guns of Corregidor controlling access to Manila Bay, hold off an enemy indefinitely. Capt. Clark knew that they were woefully undermanned, undertrained and under equipped and in their present state of readiness, it would be difficult to hold the enemy at bay for six months.

When Capt. Clark finished reading the Philippine defense plan he leaned back in his chair and reflected on how troubling the past year had been. Germany had rolled across Denmark, Norway and France. Then in September, Japan had signed the Tripartite Treaty with Germany and Italy, which meant that if the United States got drawn into the conflict in Europe, it would also be at war with Japan. To slow Japan's aggression in China, President Roosevelt had placed an embargo against Japan on oil and scrap metal, further straining relations between the two countries. There had been warnings that the Japanese planned an attack against American forces, quite possibly in the Philippines and many believed it wasn't a matter of "if" but "when."

That a Japanese attack could occur at any time made Capt. Clark's job of getting his men combat ready even more important. His father's favorite assessment of the politicians in Washington…"they don't know shit from shineola"…fit the men of A Battery perfectly. He wasn't naïve enough to believe he and his men would be the difference between victory and defeat but he was raised and trained to do the best you could with what you had. It distressed him to see that most of his fellow officers put little stock in the threat reports, still viewing the army as a "good old boys club" whose daily life revolved around the Officer's Club. He knew there was a well-trained and well-equipped enemy out there…the Japanese Imperial Army.

* * *

Since learning they were going to the Philippines, Jack and his buddies believed they were getting cushy peacetime duty in a tropical paradise, where they'd finish their hitches without being involved in any fighting. But, they were no sooner settled in their new quarters when Capt.

Clark and Sgt. Malloy launched an intensive training program that made them wonder that maybe they were wrong. They spent long hours on the rifle range, marched for miles with full packs, practiced hand-to-hand combat against each other, rammed their bayonets into dummies with a Jap face painted on them, went through endless dry runs with their anti-aircraft guns, and fell exhausted into their bunks every night. Saturday nights were their only chance to enjoy all of the pretty girls and glittery bars in Manila.

* * *

Although Jack wasn't the oldest in his circle of friends-Bobby was at least a year older-he had gradually assumed a kind of "den mother" role to the others and could generally steer them clear of trouble. One Saturday night, however, after a particularly arduous week they were in a Manila waterfront bar when Dick slammed his empty beer bottle to the table and said, "Lets all go get a tattoo."

The juke box was blaring "Tuxedo Junction," on the small dance floor where a couple of sailors were jitterbugging with two Filipino whores, and a noisy argument was going on at a pool table in the rear of the room.

At first Jack thought the beer was dulling his senses and he hadn't heard Dick correctly. "Did you say *tattoo*?"

"That's what I said," Dick replied.

"My daddy would disown me if I came home with a tattoo," said Enos. "Sheriff Conners arrested every boy he saw with a tattoo just because he figured they were guilty of something."

Dick leaned across the table, causing an empty bottle to clatter to the floor.

"Enos, my boy, maybe you haven't noticed yet but we ain't in the piney woods of Georgia anymore. And Sheriff Corners-"

"Conners," Enos corrected.

"Well shit, Enos, whatever the fuck his name is. What I was trying to say was that Sheriff Corners-"

"Conners."

"Enos, shut the fuck up."

"Well, nearly everyone I've ever seen that has a damn tattoo is a bum up to no good."

"Shit, Enos, see that Jar Head up there at the bar? See that *Semper Fi* tattooed on that great big fucking arm? Well, why don't you just ankle on up there and call him a bum up to no good. You do that and that big fucker will drive your pointy little head right through that mahogany bar, and I'll just sit here and watch. You're just chicken. You're just 'fraid it might hurt a little bit."

The Marine gunnery sergeant at the bar turned and looked over at the table with a hard glare and they all quickly looked away. He was big with a square jaw and a nose that looked like it had been through many a barroom brawl. There were five of them and only one of him, but they all knew not to start trouble with this guy.

Dick asked in a whisper that Jack could barely hear, "Think he heard me?"

"Who's chicken now?" Enos said. "Chicken, chicken, chicken. "He just looks your way and you almost shit in your pants. Chicken shit, chicken shit."

"Enos, I'm gonna come across this table and kick your ass if you don't shut up."

"Both you guys shut up," Bobby said trying to stop the bickering. "How could anybody hear you with all the noise in this place."

"Anyway, I think we outta go get tattoos," Dick said. "I saw a place right down the street."

"Let's go do it," Bobby said.

Trying to get more support, Dick turned to Buster. "How about it, Buster?"

Buster was slouched in his chair and hadn't taken his eyes off the cute Filipino whore the sailor was twirling around the dance floor. Without looking up, he said, "Sounds good to me."

Turning to Jack, Dick said, "Whadya say, Jack? We're supposed to be big bad-ass fighting men of The US Army. You gotta have a tattoo or two."

"He's right," Bobby added. "All the jar heads got em. All the swabies got em. I'm with Dickey Boy. We need em too."

On any other night Jack probably would have taken the same view as Enos, but the beer had severely clouded his judgment. Rising unsteadily to his feet with a silly grin on his face, he said, "Well, shit, let's just go do it."

The next morning, Jack awoke with a foul taste in his mouth. The blood pounded in his head with such force that he was sure his skull would burst, spewing brains all over the barracks. When he raised his head from the pillow, the walls spun around like he was on a merry-go-around. It was the first real hangover he'd ever had and couldn't believe he had gotten so drunk. He couldn't even remember getting back to the barracks. The air had the order of stale vomit and nearby he could hear someone snoring loudly. Dangling one leg over the edge of the bed, he hoped the solid floor would make the spinning room settle down. Gradually parts of the previous night began to come to him. The noisy bar, Bobby trying to get in the pants of that cute Filipino girl, the tattoo parlor. He could feel a slight sting on his left arm. There on his biceps was a beautiful American eagle in red, white and blue, clutching a bundle of arrows in its claw and holding a scroll in its beak with the words "E Pluribus Unum" inscribed on it. Boy oh boy, he thought, I've really done it now. What would his dad, think about this?

* * *

By the end of September, it was easy to see that something was afoot. Although their primary mission was anti-aircraft protection for Fort William McKinley and nearby Nichols Field, the men were being trucked several hours north, where they joined men from other units preparing defensive positions around San Fernando, the town straddling the main road into the Bataan Peninsula. Building the earthen and sandbag breastworks was hot, backbreaking work and done with such urgency that it made all of their past training easy in comparison.

"Man, this is shit," Dick said. "I didn't join the damn Army to shovel dirt. I joined the damn Army to fight."

"Looks like that's exactly what they're getting ready for us to do," said Bobby.

"Well, if we're gonna have to fight, I'd rather do it on the beaches," Dick countered. "I'd rather fight out where I can see what I'm doing."

The last few months had transformed Enos. When they arrived in the Philippines, he was a shy, slow-talking, naïve country boy who had never drunk anything stronger than apple cider, never smoked a cigarette, or uttered any oath worse than "gosh darn." Now he did all three...and even had a tattoo that Sheriff Conners would disapprove of.

Enos looked around at Dick. "I never heard such bullshit. Everybody knows you'll jump up and haul ass at the first sign of trouble."

"Go fuck yourself."

"Right back at you, Dickey Boy."

"I just know we'd be better off fighting on the beaches than we would here in this shit eating jungle."

"Dick, you don't know dick about it." With a big grin, Enos looked around at the others to make sure his clever play on words had been heard by everyone.

"Look, Enos The Penis, I know a hell of a lot more about it than you do. You 'Georgia crackers' still think the only reason the south didn't beat us Yankees was cause you ran out of collard greens and grits."

Enos, fists clinched, glared at Dick. He hated to be called "Cracker."

Dick sensing he'd gone to far, "Just forget it."

* * *

Standing at the rail of the troop transport, Kenji Tanaka could see at least a dozen vessels and knew that there were many more that he couldn't see. They had sat stationary in Japan's Inland Sea for more than two weeks while the armada was assembled and now they were finally moving. The Inland Sea was a perfect haven to gather this vast force. Surrounded by three of Japan's major islands it was impossible for anyone outside the Japanese military to know what was taking place. Surprise was a major element of the coming operations, and it had been made clear that anyone leaking word of the plans would be dealt with harshly.

Kenji thought of Takeo, who was somewhere in the north Pacific on the *Akagi*. Ever since the war games, which used the United States naval forces at Pearl Harbor as their primary objective, it was widely speculated that the First Air Fleet's mighty force would make this vital U.S. outpost its first objective. The Second Fleet, of which the ship Kenji was on was a part, was moving south with operations planned against the Philippines and other areas of Indochina. On one occasion, a British reconnaissance aircraft passed overhead and, in an effort to conceal their real intentions, the task force turned and traveled north for a time before turning back south towards its real destination.

But as slow as their progress seemed, Kenji was glad to be moving. He was sharing a small cabin with three other officers, while the enlisted men were crowded into space below decks. Conditions like this could be demoralizing. He didn't want to be leading a group of demoralized men when they landed on the beaches of Luzon where they expected fierce resistance from the American and Filipino armies.

A fellow officer, Lt. Koichi Sato, joined Kenji at the rail, and they both stared in silence at the ships plowing through the gently rolling sea.

Koichi was the first to speak. "I can hardly wait to get into action."

With a bemused look, Kenji turned to his young friend and asked, "Why?"

"It's what all Japanese men live for. It's the tradition of The Samurai."

This had been a constant theme extolled by the instructors in military school, but Kenji wondered why differences between nations couldn't be settled without death and destruction.

"You know, many men will die, don't you? Maybe even you and I?" said Kenji.

"But they will mostly be Americans. And, if you and I die, then we will know that it was an honorable death for an honorable cause. I like you, Kenji, and you're a good officer, but sometimes I don't understand you. You don't think like the other officers I know."

CHAPTER 5

Christmas was over two weeks away, but because it took that much time for their mail to reach home, Jack and Charlie went to the PX to buy Christmas cards. The tropical climate made it difficult for Jack to believe it was December 8, but he could imagine people back home warming themselves around gas heaters after being exposed to the cold north winds that blow through Texas in December. This was his first Christmas away from home, and for the first time he felt homesick. His close-knit family always gathered at Christmas. Sometimes there would be as many as thirty kinfolk at his parents house for Christmas dinner. Other years they would gather at a relative's house, eating until they could eat no more, exchanging presents, and, if the weather was good, having an impromptu game of touch football. Those were good times and it was usually the only time during the year he got to see his cousin Lonnie who, after spending their younger years like brothers, had moved to west Texas.

Charlie and Jack lingered in the PX, thumbing through magazines, buying cigarettes, and trying to decide on gifts to send home. Jack finally decided upon a little heart-shaped silver locket for Laura. As they walked out a little after noon, they heard muffled booms from the direction of Nichols Field, the Army Air Corps base adjacent to McKinley.

"What was that?" Charlie asked.

"Sounded like explosions."

As they looked toward the sounds, a plume of black smoke rose above the trees and moved by the gentle breeze, began to spread along the horizon.

"Look at all that smoke. Something must have blown up over there, said Charlie. Suddenly, two fighter aircraft with solid blood red circles on their fuselage and bottom of their wings roared overhead. Jack and Charlie stood trans-fixed as puffs of white smoke came from the wings. Then, as if everything was happening in slow motion, they heard the unmistakable chatter of machine guns.

"Shit, those Japs are shooting at us!" said Charlie. Everyone fell flat to the ground, as a stream of bullets passed perilously close over their prone bodies. Looking up Jack could see the pilot looking down at him. Then just as suddenly as they had appeared, the fighters disappeared behind a row of buildings. Jack and Charlie jumped up and sprinted to the shelter of nearby trees and, when they looked back up the road, one man still lay where he had fallen when he failed to escape the deadly hail of fire.

Jack ran back to the fallen soldier and when he rolled him over blood covered the front of his shirt. Blood trickled out the side of his mouth, and sand stuck to his face where he had pitched forward as the bullets tore into his back. Jack could only stare, as he realized what had happened. For months they had trained and prepared for war, but could any man be prepared to see his first casualty?

* * *

Capt. Clark was in his office talking to Sgt. Malloy when the attack came. Rushing outside they saw the Japanese fighters flying just above the treetops. They had spent considerable time setting up their guns to protect McKinley and Nichols and, as they raced down the road to where their battery was set up, they could see that the training was paying off. The guns were firing rapidly at streaking fighters.

When a formation of Japanese bombers came into view, the gun crews swiveled around to fire at the approaching aircraft. In minutes all of the guns were firing as fast as the men could slam a shell into the breech and pull the lanyard. They fired in defense of their lives. And they fired in anger at an enemy who without warning had rained death and destruction down on them. But the guns were largely ineffective against the high-flying bombers, the shells exploding well below the bombers.

Jack and Charlie reached their gun as a second wave of bombers came into view and soon joined the battle. The bombers seemed immune to the barrage of exploding shells but a cheer went up when one of the attacking aircraft broke from formation, smoke trailing from one of its engines. They watched its deadly spiral until the doomed craft disappeared behind the trees and a column of black smoke rose into the sky.

The enemy continued their attacks for nearly three hours and Jack could see smoke rising from Nichols Field where he knew aircraft were parked. In the distance, enemy bombers circled Manila and Jack could hear muffled explosions from the direction of the defenseless city. A number of bombs fell close to A Battery's position, and

Jack saw his second casualty of the war when the gun next to his was showered with flying pieces of shrapnel and a piece of hot metal tore through Bobby's shoulder.

When the raids ended, a jeep roared up and skidded to a stop.

"Capt. Clark, Col. Moore wants all battery commanders up at Regiment right away," the driver yelled. As Clark climbed in the back seat, he called out to Lt. Henry Zimmerman, one of his platoon leaders, "Henry, keep the men on the alert. We might have another wave anytime."

"OK let's go," he said to the driver. The jeeps rear wheels spun in the gravel and sped off in the direction of Regimental Headquarters.

The first person Capt. Clark saw as he entered the briefing room was Maj. Tim Brown. A classmate at West Point, Tim was a rising star, having been promoted to Major far ahead of his classmates, and was now the Regimental Executive Officer. The normally quiet headquarters was total bedlam, with people rushing around, papers in hand, some talking on phones and others just standing around with bewildered looks on their faces. The packed room was filled with loud, excited talk as each man told his version of the surprise attack and speculating as to what was taking place.

"Officers, attention," Maj. Brown called as the door opened and Col. Ed Moore walked to a podium at the front of the room. Behind him was a large map of the Philippines.

As the room grew quite, Col Moore spoke. "As you all know Japan has attacked us. Although I have not received official notification, I assume that we are at war. The attacks were widespread and have also been carried out against Clark Field, Cavite, and Subic Bay. All have been heavily damaged. We lost most of the B-17's and P-40's on the ground, but a few fighters did get airborne. Six Jap planes were shot down."

With a grim expression and unmistakable anger, he continued. "I have also received word that there were simultaneous attacks against Pearl Harbor, causing great loss of life. The Pacific Fleet and all other installations in Hawaii have suffered heavy damage, which puts us in a tough spot." A low murmur filled the room as Col. Moore scanned the concerned faces. "If the Japs control the Pacific, we could very well be stuck out here with no way to get supplies or reinforcements. Until we know otherwise, that means we must use our resources-and I'm talking about personnel as well as materials-in the most efficient manner possible."

A wave of guilt swept over Col. Moore as he looked at the faces before him. He already knew the Philippines would never receive more supplies or reinforcements. Their sole mission was to buy time so that the Pacific Fleet could be rebuilt and strike back at the enemy.

"Now for the good news. As far as I know Japanese forces haven't landed here or in Hawaii, but I think we can expect these raids to be followed up at some time by ground operations."

Col. Moore paused. "With that in mind I trust each of you are up to speed on our defense plans. If not, get familiar with them real fast. Any questions?"

Hands shot up all over the room.

* * *

"Kenji, did you hear?" Koichi rushed through the door of the small cabin he and two other officers shared with Kenji.

"We've bombed Pearl Harbor and all the American bases in the Philippines. They say the destruction is so complete that the war will be over in three months."

"Did we suffer any losses?" Kenji immediately thought of Takeo who he was sure would have been in the initial attack.

"Only three or four aircraft out of the hundreds used in the attacks. It was a total victory. The American dogs were completely humiliated."

"It's hard to believe the Americans were so ill prepared."

"Come, let's go see what else they are saying." Excitedly, Koichi took Kenji by the arm,

The companionways were crowded, and like waves crashing on a beach, cheers rolled through the companionways as word of the great victory spread. When Kenji reached the officers' wardroom, it was filled with men whose boredom was suddenly replaced with an eagerness to get into the fray and show that the Imperial Army was the mightiest military force in the world.

Suddenly the speaker mounted on the wardroom wall crackled and came to life with the voice of General Homma.

"Brave warriors of Japan, today a great victory was scored over forces of the United States and the British Empire. This was not a war we sought, but one we were forced to undertake because of the unfair and intransigent policies these nations were pursuing against us. The victories we achieved today assure us of total control over the entire Pacific and Indochina. Now we can take our rightful place among the world's great nations. Soon you will be called on to conduct ground operations against the American and Filipino forces on the Island of Luzon...*and we will be victorious.*"

The cheers were deafening and, despite his misgivings, Kenji's spine tingled with excitement. He could see himself leading his men through the foaming surf and up the white beaches as the sand sprouted with the impact of the enemies' bullets. *Bushido*, the ancient code of the Samurai, filled his heart...death before dishonor, and an absolute willingness to accept death if he could advance the goals of the Japanese Empire.

CHAPTER 6

After the initial raids on December 8, enemy aircraft returned every day for the next two weeks. Sometimes, the guns would get so hot that they'd jam and had to cool before they would fire again. The men of A Battery did their best to ward off the endless stream of enemy planes, but their old shells would often misfire. An entire gun crew in B Battery was killed when an ill-fitting shell exploded in the gun's breech. More ammo had to arrive soon or they would be defenseless.

The Japanese raids were devastating, and casualties mounted. The fighters would come in fast and low making it impossible to swivel the guns fast enough to keep the aircraft in their sights. Sandbags stacked around the gun positions did little to stop the shrapnel. Jack and Charlie had come through unscathed so far, but A Battery had suffered three dead and eight wounded the first week of raids. Bobby had survived and had been taken to a hospital at Clark.

Most of the aircraft at Nichols had been destroyed, and after the first day no American airplane had been seen airborne. The fuel dump had taken a direct hit, and black smoke billowed over the land like a black funeral shroud. Many buildings at McKinley and Nichols had been destroyed; not a single one had escaped damage.

As Jack and Charlie sat by their gun after the latest raid, Charlie said, "Why in hell do they keep coming back? There ain't' nothing left to bomb." As Jack looked out over the post, he had to agree. It looked as if some giant creature had stomped through, smashing a building flat here, kicking another into splinters there. Where before there had been orderly rows of buildings, now there was only piles of shattered wood. Only the runways at Nichols were spared, an ominous sign because it was believed the Japanese would use them when the Philippines fell-and the way it looked, that wouldn't be long in coming.

Fourteen days after the first attacks, word swept through the ranks that the Japs had landed on the beaches of Northern Luzon. Although everyone had expected it, it was still a shock to realize they might soon be under attack by expert soldiers so dedicated that they would gladly die before accepting defeat.

"Man, I sure wish I'd learned to use this damn M-1 better." Charlie cradled the gun in his hands. They had been given limited training on the rifle range, and Enos was the only one among them who had received a sharpshooters badge. Being a good shooter came natural to Enos. His father had given him a single-shot 22 when he was six. By the time he was seven he could knock a squirrel out of a tree with a single shot to the head. By way of explaining his marksmanship, he say, "You had to be good with a single shot .22 cause you never got a second chance."

"Well, when I got in the artillery, I didn't know I'd have to fight with some damn rifle?" said Dick, as they rested between raids, their backs propped against sandbags.

Jack, always the optimist, said, "Quit worrying so much. Fresh troops are probably on the way right now. And besides that we've still got Corregidor, which means they can land reinforcements in Manila any time they want."

"Shit, Jack, where do you think they're gonna come from?" said Dick. "You know damn well that we probably don't have a damn ship in the whole fucking Pacific that ain't already been sunk."

Within hours of hearing of the Japanese landing, American and Filipino troops began heading north to establish new defensive lines.

* * *

The landings on the beaches of Luzon went almost unopposed, and now Kenji, as a part of General Homma's main force, was moving rapidly down Route 5 toward Manila. They had broken through stubborn American resistance at Cabanatuan, and their next objective was to capture the two bridges that crossed the Pampanga River at Calumpit.

The relative ease of the landings disappointed the young officers in Kenji's unit. Eager to demonstrate their bravery in the face of enemy fire, they saw the enemy's unwillingness to fight as another insult from the arrogant Americans. Many had leaped from the landing craft, brandishing their swords, only to be cut down by the sparse but accurate enemy fire. But any thoughts that victory would be easy were soon dispelled when they attacked Cabanatuan. The Americans fought with great courage against overwhelming odds, but after several days of intense fighting, retreated toward the vital bridges over the Pampanga River. Now the Japanese forces had the Americans on the run.

Intelligence revealed just how important the Calumpit bridges were to the Americans. Gen. MacArthur's plan was to withdraw all his forces into the Bataan Peninsula until help arrived. To do this, all the American forces around Manila would have to cross the bridges and, if the Japanese army could gain control before all had crossed, the American and Filipino forces would be split in half. They also knew that the Americans would make another strong stand somewhere north of the bridges, probably at the towns of Baliuag and a few miles further south at Plaridal.

Kenji and Koichi rode in the cab and in the rear of the big truck were twenty combat troops under their command. With his usual bluster, Koichi said, " I hope the American dogs turn and fight soon so we can end this war and be home by the New Year."

"That's one of the dumbest things you've ever said," said Kenji. "You saw how they fought at Cabanatuan. They were completely outnumbered but they still held us off for three days."

"Well, I heard that Tojo said that the war would be over in three months at the most."

"I hope he is correct."

Kenji's doubts about his country's militaristic attitude had grown even greater when he saw his first combat death. He would never forget the sight. A lieutenant he had come to know quite well had been leading his men across the beach when an enemy bullet hit him squarely between the eyes. The man's head snapped back and exploded in a red mist that showered Kenji with blood and brain. As Kenji looked down at the lifeless face-mouth agape and eyes frozen open-he thought he looked, except for the small red hole right on the bridge of his nose, just as he did when they stood on the ship's deck before landing. Then he had been an exuberant young warrior waving his white scarf and shouting *Bonzai.* Now he lay dead on a white beach far from home.

* * *

On the afternoon of the December 30, Gen. Jonathan Wainwright, the American Commander of the forces in Northern Luzon, ordered Col. Moore and his regiment to move north and set up defensive positions at the barrio of Baliuag. The village lay squarely in the path of the Japanese advance down Route 5 toward the Calumpit bridges. Everyone understood the importance of stopping the Japanese advance. If the Japanese could destroy the bridges the Philippines were lost.

Hitching their guns to the heavy trucks, the men of A battery knew they would be exposed to enemy aircraft while moving up the narrow highway. If caught in the open, they would suffer heavy losses. The only consolation was that it would be dark in a few hours and the Japanese planes rarely operated at night.

Only once during the trip north did they see any Japanese planes and they were at high altitude, apparently headed for another pounding of Manila. All troops had been pulled out of Manila and the city had been declared an "open city" by Gen. MacArthur, but the Japanese continued their relentless bombing. Passing through Manila they were shocked to see the once dynamic city virtually destroyed. No pretty girls waved from the curb. Only a few dazed people picked through the rubble that had once been their homes.

To get to their position at Baliuag, the regiment had to cross the bridges at Calumpit, then travel north up Route 5 to Baliuag. As they crossed the two bridges that spanned the Pampanga engineers could be seen climbing through the bridge beams attaching explosive charges.

Charlie turned to Jack, "Do you see what I see? They're fixing to blow these damn bridges."

"Yeah," Enos said, "and we're going to be on the wrong side of the river.

"You guys do a lot of talking about something you don't know anything about," Jack said. Hell, I bet they never have to blow them. Look at everything we got going up the road. We'll stop the Japs before they ever get here."

"Why in the hell they putting out explosives then?" Enos asked.

"Just getting ready in case worse comes to worse."

"Glad you've got so much confidence in the U.S. Army, Jack. They been promising us more men and ammo for weeks, and I ain't seen one damn man or bullet yet," said Dick.

Jack really didn't have that much confidence either. He just had to show a brave face, hoping to keep the other's morale up. It was true they hadn't received reinforcements or ammo, but he wasn't ready to give up hope yet

CHAPTER 7

They all considered it a miracle that they reached
Baliuag without being caught in the open by Japanese
bombers. After reaching Route 5, they joined a long column of infantry being moved into position to stop the
Japanese and their progress slowed to a crawl.

Baliuag was a small town of houses and nipa huts
spread along the banks of the Angat River. Japanese bombers had destroyed the bridge and one section slanted into
the river like a playground slide, but the Angat, smaller
than the Pampanga, could easily be forded. The 201st set
up its guns west of town, where they could fire on the road
leading into Baliuag and on likely crossing points for the
Japanese forces.

Darkness brought little relief from the heat and Jack's
shirt, soaked with perspiration, clung to his body. The slow
moving vehicles had stirred up clouds of dust that clogged
his throat and made his eyes feel like they were filled with
ground glass. After they reached Baliuag, Capt. Clark and
Sgt. Malloy pushed them to set up their guns, and it was
after sunrise before they could rest.

Too keyed up to sleep, Jack lay under the gun and watched the trees on the far side of the Angat. They had been at war for almost a month now, enduring countless air attacks but, up until now, the enemy had been some remote, sinister figure crouched in a cockpit peering through a gun sight. Now for the first time, he might come face to face with someone intent on ending his life.

"Charlie, you asleep?"

"Naw. I'm too damn tired to sleep. Ever get that way?"

"Yeah, I'm the same way,"

Charlie was silent for a moment and then asked, "Know what day it is?" Before Jack could answer, Charlie said, "It's New Years Day. Never thought I'd be spending it lying under some damn gun in the middle of nowhere, waiting for some slant- eyed son of a bitch to stick a bayonet up my ass. You scared?"

"I wouldn't be human if I wasn't," Jack said. "How bout you?"

"I ain't human then. When you grow up with an old man who got drunk on Jax beer every night and beat you up just for the hell of it, you learn it don't do no good to be scared. What's gonna happen is gonna happen and there ain't a damn thing you can do about it." Then with a chuckle, "With Malloy on our side, the damn Japs are the ones that better be scared."

Jack was silent for a minute, and then said, "Yeah I guess you're right. I've never been a real religious guy, but at a time like this you need a little faith. Maybe the man upstairs has it all planned out for us...you know, pre-ordained destiny."

"Like I said, what's gonna happen is gonna happen."

Jack's first opportunity to rest in more than 24 hours was short-lived. In a cloud of dust a jeep skidded to a stop and Lt. Zimmerman shouted, "Collins. They want you up at Col. Moore's command post. Get in."

Jack climbed into the rear seat and the jeep sped off. Entering a small grove of trees, Jack saw Col. Moore, Capt. Clark, and several other officers bent over a map spread out on the hood of a Jeep. As Jack got out of the Jeep, Capt. Clark turned and said, "Col. Moore, this is Private Collins."

Jack had only seen Col. Moore from a distance...as the he went by in his jeep or when they marched on the parade ground and the command "eyes right" was given. Now, up close, Jack could see Col. Moore was a handsome man, his black hair sprinkled with gray and a pencil-thin mustache above a firm mouth.

Col. Moore returned Jack's salute. "Private Collins. Capt. Clark said you were his best artillery spotter in training. Think you can do that good a job under real combat conditions.?"

"Yes sir. I believe I can."

"Good. Go with Corp. Lucas here, and be our forward observer so we can get some accurate fire on the enemy when they try to cross the river. Look at the map here."

As Jack and Lucas bent over the map, Col. Moore pointed, "Set up your observation post right here on the crest of this hill. Take these binoculars and this radio and as soon as you see any Japs, let us know. Now get going."

Jack put his arms through the straps attached to the radio and hoisted it on his back, as Lucas took the map from Col. Moore.

Jack drove as Lucas studied the map. The hill Col. Moore had pointed out rose high above the town's south side. When they were in position, they had a commanding view of the destroyed bridge, the river in both directions and the entire village. North of the bridge the road disappeared into the dense jungle.

As they lay watching, Jack was aware that an eerie calm had settled over the scene...as if the world was holding its breath. The jungle birds and animals seemed to know that their world would soon erupt in death and destruction, and had retreated to safety. The small town below them was still and silent, with no indication that it might still be occupied.

It was strange the way they appeared. Jack had screwed off the cap of his canteen and taken a long swig of the cool water while Lucas fiddled with the radio. Wiping his mouth with the back of his hand, Jack looked toward the bridge. Only moments before the road had been empty, but now there was a small group of Japanese standing in the road.

Jack nudged Lucas with his elbow. "Luke, look there."

As they watched, two tanks emerged from the forest, stopping behind the group of soldiers.

Lucas spoke rapidly into the microphone, "We've got enemy troops and tanks on the road north of the bridge."

Col. Moore took the microphone from his radioman and replied, "Lucas. You've got to do better than that. How many tanks? How far up the road?"

"The troops are about 300 meters from the bridge but not moving now. Just standing there. Looks like they're looking the situation over. We see two tanks and they're moving toward the bridge 200 meters north now."

As Jack looked through the binoculars, he could clearly see the facial features of the Japanese soldiers standing in the road...his first real look at the enemy.

Even though the Japanese were well out of hearing, Jack whispered, "Those are the first Japs I've ever seen."

"Yeah, me too. We had some chinks back home, but no Japs that I can remember."

Suddenly, the silence was broken by the *swoosh* of an artillery shell passing overhead. Jack and Lucas buried their faces in the ground, looking up only after they heard the shell's impact. It hit directly in the middle of the road, but well short of the tanks or enemy soldiers. Lucas spoke into his microphone, "Short. Azimuth good, but 50 meters short."

The Japanese scurried back into the trees, as another round passed overhead, impacting with a great flash and a cloud of black dirt. Again Lucas spoke to the gunners. "You got the tanks bracketed."

The next round spun the lead tank around, completely blowing off its left tread. Two more rounds followed in rapid succession. One hit the second tank squarely in its side. Jack was looking directly at the tank when the shell ripped a gaping hole in its side. Like a blowtorch flames shot from the turret, and Jack watched with morbid fascination as a Japanese soldier, his clothes ablaze struggled to escape the inferno. As the flames engulfed his body, the soldier's struggles slowed and finally stopped altogether. He was a Jap and he was an enemy, who would not have given a second thought to killing him or Lucas, but Jack thought that no man should have to die like that.

When more Japanese tanks came into view, the shells from the 201st guns slowed their advance but several reached the river and churned through the shallow water before being stopped by direct hits. Gray smoke spread over the town making it difficult for Jack to see what was happening. Then as the cloud thinned, he could see Japanese infantry entering the town from the east. They had forded the river upstream and were already running down the narrow streets, darting in and out buildings.

Lucas, with a slight panic in his voice, spoke into the radio. "We've got Japs in town on the east side."

The guns shifted their aim to where the Japanese soldiers were dodging from house to house when a squadron of American tanks accompanied by infantry swept into town. When Lucas reported the friendly tanks, the artillery barrage was lifted to avoid hitting the Americans. After that, Jack watched, fascinated, as the tanks and foot soldiers played their deadly game of hide and seek. The tanks wheeled through the narrow streets, smashing houses and straw huts like so many toothpicks as the infantry ducked in and out of doors and crouched behind collapsed buildings. But Jack knew it was a losing battle. Vastly outnumbered, it was only a matter of time before the Americans would have to withdraw. It had taken a lot of effort to hold this little town for such a short time, but everyone knew the importance of keeping the bridges at Calumpit open. Every hour they were open meant that thousands of American and Filipino soldiers could escape to the safety of Bataan.

* * *

Lt. Kenji Tanaka's unit had been ordered to circle to the east and attack the enemy's flank where the defenses were the weakest. Crossing where the river was shallow they swept down on the town and entered its eastern edge, drawing only sporadic artillery fire from the American guns. But American tanks soon come rampaging through the town like wild elephants, smashing everything in their path. The rifle fire did little to stop the tanks. Kenji saw one soldier climb on a tank and attempted to fire through the slits in the turret. The tank wheeled in a tight turn and the man was thrown off and crushed under the churning treads. Just when it appeared they would be driven back out of town, a unit of Japanese tanks came roaring into the battle, and with their superior numbers turned the tide.

By late afternoon the imperial army had firm control of Baliuag and American artillery fire ended when darkness fell. Around midnight, engines could be heard as the Americans withdrew back towards Calmupit.

* * *

Shortly before midnight, word came down to the 201st to start their withdrawal back down Route 5. They had been in position less than 24 hours, but the battle for Baliuag was over.

The withdrawal went smoothly with no pursuit from the Japanese. The tacticians had chosen the small town of Plaridel, south of Baliuag on Route 5, as another strategic point in the defense of the bridges at Calumpit. When the 201st reached it, Jack saw that it was already occupied by what seemed to be an entire infantry division and at least two tank battalions. The entire town was blacked out except for one building whose windows glowed with a dim yellow light. As the lead vehicle drew abreast of the building, the vehicles stopped and Col. Moore hurried toward the open door. Leaning from the truck, Charlie asked an infantry sergeant standing nearby, "What's going on up there?" The Sergeant motioned with his head toward the building and said, "That's Gen. Wainwright's HQ. The old man himself is in there."

Within minutes, Col. Moore returned to his Jeep, and the convoy resumed its journey.

Jack looked at Charlie with an obvious look of relief. "Well, I guess we're not gonna have to fight here."

* * *

In Kenji's mind, the American defense at the small town of Plaridel had been the stiffest resistance they had encountered since landing on the beaches of Luzon. The American and Filipino forces had withstood repeated attacks for the better part of two days, but had finally been overwhelmed by the superior numbers and weapons of the Japanese Army. This time the Americans had not retreated.

They had fought with remarkable bravery almost to the last man and many of the enemy still lay where they fell, the Americans not having the opportunity to bury them.

By now, Kenji had become accustomed to death and could usually put the sight of the dead out of his mind, but the body of one American soldier left a lasting impression on him. The boy, who looked no more than eighteen was propped against a tree with a small notepad and a partially written letter in his lap. He had evidently been wounded in the fighting and too weak to retreat had attempted to write a last letter home. The letter was never finished and the people for whom it was intended would never know what had happened to him. As he stood looking at the boy, he wondered why young men, with so much promise and so much life still ahead, had to die because nations couldn't settle their differences in peaceful ways?

When they finally reached the Pampanga, they found that the Americans' valiant stand had accomplished its goal: the bridges had been destroyed. This could only mean the American forces had crossed, escaping the trap and were probably now consolidating their forces in Bataan...It also meant that the door to Manila was wide open.

CHAPTER 8

As he crossed the Pampanga River Capt. Clark wondered why Japanese bombers had not already destroyed the bridges. Their destruction would have been as effective as their capture; either way, the American forces would have been split in half. But now, that opportunity had been lost and in a matter of hours all forces east of the Pampanga would be across and withdrawn into Bataan.

After going back through Calumpit, the 201st halted and set up their guns to cover approaches to the bridges. As they watched the road for any sign of the enemy, trucks, buses and foot soldiers streamed across the bridges. With Manila being threatened by the Japanese, the civilian population had begun its own exodus to Bataan adding to the congestion. Old cars, trucks, buses, ox carts, and even wheelbarrows...anything that could carry people or their meager belongings...mixed in with the military traffic making progress painfully slow.

For two days, there was no sign of the enemy, which meant that the troops at Plaridel were holding the Japanese at bay. Around midnight of the second day, however, vehicles loaded with men, many wounded, trickled in from the direction of Plaridel with word that they had finally been overrun.

When Gen. Wainwright, was informed that the last troops were safely across he ordered the bridges blown. With a tremendous roar both bridges collapsed into the river. After their destruction the 201st and an infantry division dug in on the west side of the river to make the Japanese crossing as difficult as possible.

Col. Moore summoned his battery commanders together. Looking slowly from man to man, he studied their faces to see how they were holding up under the constant pressure. "All right men, we've got a job to do and not a hell of a lot to do it with." With a wave toward the river, he continued. "The Japs will be coming down that road and will try to cross that river and we're going to make damn sure they pay a heavy price doing it."

The men were silent as they waited for him to continue. "We don't have a lot of ammo, and we're outnumbered, but by God we're still the U.S. Army and we're going to make it tough on those bastards. Pick your targets carefully. Make your aim good.. Make every round count. And let's show those S. O B's. some real fighting men.."

Soon after the meeting with Moore, Japanese forces were sighted approaching the river. The Pampanga would be a much greater obstacle for the Japanese than the smaller Angat River at Baliuag. With its width, depth, and swift current, Capt. Clark knew they could slow the enemy's advance, but he was also realistic enough to know that sooner or later the superior numbers of the Japanese would prevail and they would be forced to retreat once again.

As he moved among the gun positions, he stopped and talked to each gun crew, repeating what Col. Moore had said in an attempt to boost moral. But he needn't have worried. As he moved among the men he realized that moral was remarkably high, considering their desperate situation.

"Good job spotting back there, Collins," he said when he walked up to Jack's gun.

"Thank you, Sir."

"We won't need any forward observers here," Capt. Clark said. "We have a clear line of sight on anyone trying to get across the river. We're going to hit them at the edge of the river but be sure to get your range right because we have infantry down there on this side."

As they looked down at the river, the first shot of the battle of the Calumpit bridges was fired when a Japanese artillery shell slammed into the infantry troops along the riverbank. A steady barrage followed as Japanese tanks and foot soldiers tried to reach the river. The big guns and infantry firing from their defensive positions along the riverbank took a heavy toll and soon the far bank was littered with dead and wounded Japanese soldiers. But there was just to many and eventually the first Japanese soldiers, followed by several tanks, were able to cross on portable pontoon bridges and gained a foothold on the west bank.

As Capt. Clark watched the action, he realized that someone without an overall knowledge of the situation would think the American forces were winning this battle. The Japanese dead and wounded outnumbered those on the U.S. side by at least ten to one, but still the Japanese were achieving their goal of getting across the river. In his military science courses back at the Point, he had been taught that if you achieved your goal, you had won. Losses mattered, and you hated to lose one single man, but in war, first and foremost you must achieve your objective.

* * *

Lt. Kenji Tanaka and his unit of infantry remained concealed in the trees while the artillery pounded the Americans defending the river.

As he watched the earth boil up in great clouds of dirt, he didn't see how anyone could survive such a bombardment. But survive they did, and when he was ordered to advance his men to the river's edge, they came under withering fire. Leading his men down the sloping ground, Kenji sprinted for the shelter of a concrete pillar still standing at the waters' edge. The whine of bullets sounded like a swarm of angry bees, and he could hear a dull *splat* when they found their mark in human flesh. When he was safely behind the pillar, he looked back and saw many of his men lying dead and wounded. Those that reached the river had little shelter from the deadly fire and crouched behind the slightest rise in the terrain. Some, unable to find any other protection, lay prone behind the bodies of their fallen comrades.

Seeing so many of his men killed and wounded pained Kenji, but he knew that their sacrifice would ensure victory. When one fell, another took his place, and the fire from the Americans on the opposite bank grew less intense as the day wore on. By afternoon, despite the fearful toll from the American fire, the Japanese soldiers were able to cross the river and begin to drive the enemy back once again.

* * *

The order to withdraw came at 5 p.m. The 201st was to move up Route 3 to San Fernando, where it intersected Route 7, the main road into the Bataan Peninsula. Holding the crossroads at San Fernando would give MacArthur time to move all his forces into Bataan. But time was running out.

Enemy bombers were a constant threat, and each time they came into view, the trucks would drive off the road seeking shelter under the trees. The retreating men would scramble to find shelter, but there was never enough for everyone and men would be forced to fall flat in an open area, shielding their heads with their arms as if that were enough to stop a piece of red-hot shrapnel.

Jack soon learned that the only way to keep his sanity was to believe that it would never happen to him. One time when an aircraft came into view and everyone found what cover they could, white pieces of paper- leaflets urging the Americans to surrender-instead of bombs floated down. The men stuffed the paper in their pockets using them to light cigarettes, write notes to the people at home, and as a substitute for toilet paper, a luxury they hadn't had in weeks.

As the 201st joined a defensive line being formed south of San Fernando, Jack realized that the war had settled into a disturbing routine-fight for as long as you could, fall back, dig in, fight some more-and then start the process all over again. Without fuel to keep all of the trucks running, many, along with the guns they were pulling, were abandoned. The trucks would be burned, tires slashed, wiring ripped out and fuel tanks punctured to make sure the enemy couldn't use them. The guns were wortless without the proper shells.

As A Battery set up its newest position, a Jeep came up and Bobby, who had been wounded the first day, jumped out.

"Hey guys, look who's here," Enos shouted.

They gathered around, slapping Bobby on the back and shaking his hand.

"Glad to see you decided to help us fight these damn Japs," Dick teased.

"Hey Bobby, how were those nurses?" Buster grinned.

"They all wore combat boots and baggy fatigues…you couldn't even tell if they had tits," said Bobby.

"Don't give us that shit, Bobby. I'll bet you talked at least one of them into boosting the morale of a wounded hero," Dick retorted

Bobby just gave them a sly look that only confirmed in Enos' mind that Bobby, who had a reputation as a real ladies man, had indeed cut a wide swath through the ranks of nurses at some field hospital.

The new defensive position proved to be tougher for the Japanese to crack because, for the first time, the entire American and Filipino force had come together to form a consolidated front. The fighting gradually settled into a battle of attrition. The Americans and Filipinos had as many men as the Japanese, but they were woefully short of the supplies-ammunition, medicine, clothing, fuel, and, most of all, food. Jack now understood what the saying "an army fights on its stomach" meant. They had been on half rations since the withdrawal from Calumpit and their daily ration was a small amount of rice, with canned milk and sugar, a can of sardines, or, if they were lucky, a can of salmon and sometimes a piece of bread for each meal. The lack of an adequate diet affected not only their strength but their morale as well.. But Jack soon learned how resourceful desperate men can be when faced with starvation...they ate rats, lizards, monkeys, *anything.* One day, an Army mule wandered into the area and ended up a sumptuous feast for the hungry men. Dysentery and malaria were taking almost as heavy a toll as the Japanese, and some were too weak to walk. But they fought on and what's more they fought well.

Both sides were suffering enormous casualties, and the Japanese paid heavily for every foot of ground they wrested from the Americans, yet they continued to force the Americans to fall farther back into the swamps and jungles of Bataan. On February 15, they were stunned to hear that Singapore had fallen to the Japanese.

Their last supply line had been lost.

A song began to circulate through the ranks:

We're the battling bastards of Bataan

No mama, no papa, no Uncle Sam

No aunts, no uncles, no nieces

No rifles, no planes, or artillery pieces

And nobody gives a damn.

Jack got by on very little sleep and had learned the trick of waking up and being instantly alert when danger was at hand, but sleeping through any noise that presented no danger. One night he awakened suddenly when a Japanese soldier, trying to creep up on their position, stepped on a dry twig, causing the slightest of sounds. Another time he slept soundly in a ditch alongside a road when a convoy of big army trucks rumbled by. Lack of sleep and meager rations began to take a toll on his body and his khakis hung loosely on his six- foot three inch frame. Nonetheless he was in better shape than a lot of the others. Charlie had malaria and was sometimes so weak that he could hardly lift his rifle. Bobby's shoulder was still bandaged and starting to ooze blood. Enos had an open sore on his arm from an infected insect bite. Buster had been wounded in the foot and limped along on a crutch fashioned from a tree branch. And Lt. Zimmerman had died leading a charge on a Japanese machine gun position that had pinned them down for hours. The brave lieutenant and the two other men worked their way close enough to lob grenades and knock out the gun, but as Jack and the other men provided covering fire, they were cut down as they ran back to safety.

After falling back once again an unexpected lull in the fighting gave the men hope that they would get some rest, but even though there were no frontal assaults the Japanese maintained constant pressure. Loud speakers would blare threats, insults and entreaties to surrender. At night as the men lay in their foxholes, nostalgic music, meant to remind the soldiers of home, played continuously; the most popular was Bing Crosby's "White Christmas." Sniper fire was a constant threat and the slightest movement would draw the deadly accurate fire and at night when the darkness allowed some movement parachute flares would streak into the sky and men caught in the open would be forced to dive to the ground.

The days went by and in early March, Capt. Clark gathered his men. "Listen up. I have something important to read you. I have a message from Gen. MacArthur, who has moved his headquarters to Corregidor."

Dick leaned close to Jack and said, "Like rats leaving a sinking ship."

Capt. Clark, looked sharply at Dick then back at the paper. "Help is on the way from the States. Thousands of troops and hundreds of planes are being dispatched. No further retreat is possible. We have more troops in Bataan than the Japanese have thrown against us. Our supplies are ample; a determined defense will defeat the enemy attack." Capt. Clark looked up then continued. "I call upon every soldier in Bataan to resist the enemy with courage and determination. This is the only road to victory. If we fight, we will win; if we retreat, we will be destroyed." At first there was only silence, then one of the men in the rear shouted, "Ample supplies. Begging your pardon, sir, but I ain't had a decent meal in two months."

Another shouted. "No more retreat? That's easy for him to say, sitting over there on Corregidor."

Capt. Clark held up his hands to quiet the men. "I know how you feel. Things are tough, but we need to hold on until reinforcements arrive. We've already heard what happens if you're captured. Believe me, you're better off dead."

Dick spoke up. "Not meaning any disrespect, Capt., but we don't believe any troops and planes are on the way. The General is just plain full of sh....bull."

Clark couldn't get angry. What the men were saying was true. Everyone in position to receive intelligence reports had known for days that reinforcements would never arrive and if the Philippines were to be held, it was up to these men to do it. He hated lying to the men but if they knew the truth, moral would plummet and the battle for the Philippines would be over.

The lull in fighting could only mean the Japanese were massing their forces for the final assault to drive the Americans and Filipinos to the very tip of Bataan from where there would be no further retreat. But they weren't prepared for the ferocity of the attack when it finally came.

Accompanied by massive artillery barrages, and constant dive-bomber attacks, wave after wave of Japanese infantry, shouting *"Bonzai!Bonzai!"* threw themselves at the American defenses. Overwhelmed, the 201st was forced to abandon their artillery altogether but continued to fight with their M-1's. The Japanese would hurl themselves on the barbed wire that had been rolled out to slow their advance, and those that followed would use the bodies as human bridges.

Once, during a lull in the fighting, Jack turned to Charlie and said, "How can you beat a people that's got no regard for human life.?"

"Just kill 'em all," said Charlie.

Jack said, "Well, the more we kill, the more they keep coming."

"I once read in Believe It or Not that if you lined the Japs up five across and they started marching past you, they'd never stop going by," said Enos

"That wasn't the damn Japs. It was the Chinese. It's not the same," said Dick.

"Their all the same to me."

That night during a heavy rain the Japanese made a wild charge at the American lines. During the height of battle, a flash of lightning illuminated the scene and Jack clearly saw a Japanese soldier standing no more than three feet away. Jack fired into the blackness and when another flash of lightning lit the scene, the man had disappeared. No shout of pain, no thud as a body hit the ground. Nothing. The sight unnerved Jack and, as the battle raged he became so confused that he wasn't sure he was firing in the right direction. Seeing a dark shadow he fired his rifle and immediately heard a gruff voice, "Hold your fire, goddam-it! I'm American."

As the confusion mounted, Jack grabbed Charlie and pulled him into some high grass where they lay quietly until the sounds of battle faded. By sunrise, a deathly silence had settled over the entire area. It was so quiet that Jack wondered if everyone-Japanese and Americans alike- had died in the battle. Certain the Japanese had overrun the American positions, he and Charlie stayed in the elephant grass until late afternoon. When Jack finally decided it was safe to move, they used the sun to guide them in the direction they thought the American forces had gone. They stopped every few minutes to listen for any sound that might mean the enemy was near. With the grass higher than his head, it was impossible for Jack to see more than a few feet and he would occasionally lift Charlie to look around.

After walking for two days, Charlie looked out over the swaying sea of grass. "I see some trucks over there with some guys standing around."

"They might be Japanese." Jack quickly lowered Charlie. "Did they see you?"

"I don't think so, but I think they're our guys."

"How do you know?"

"One don't have no helmet on and he looked blond to me-I ain't never seen a blond Jap."

Moving in the direction Charlie had seen the men they came to the edge of a road and Jack carefully parted the grass. Not twenty feet away, four American GI's stood smoking and talking beside a mud splattered, army truck.

Walking out of the grass with their hands raised Jack said, "Any you fellows know where the 201st Artillery is? Me and my buddy got separated during that last battle."

A short, wiry, man stepped forward. His weathered face had a stubble of dark beard and he was so deeply tanned it was difficult to tell, until he spoke, whether he was American or Filipino.

"The 201st? Were they up at McKinley?"

"That's right. You seen 'em?"

"No, but if there's any left, they got to be up ahead somewhere. They sure as hell ain't nothing behind us except the damn Japs."

When the man raised his arm to point up the road, Jack saw the tattoo on his forearm, "The Raging Cajun."

"There's Japs no more a mile up there." Then he added, "I'm Sgt. LeBeau, and you can hitch with us till we find your outfit."

A lieutenant with a map in his hand emerged from behind the truck. "OK, LeBeau, let's get moving."

LeBeau turned to Jack and said, "This here is Lt. Carson." Turning back to Carson he said, "Lieutenant, these guys got separated from their outfit and I told them they could hitch up with us."

"Sure, that's no problem." Looking at Charlie. "What's wrong with you, soldier?"

Charlie stood there with his arms crossed tightly across his chest, trying vainly to hold back the shakes that gripped his body.

"He's got a bad case of malaria and can hardly walk," said Jack.

Lt. Carson motioned to a couple of the men, "Put him in the truck. We need to get moving."

"What unit did you say you were from?" Carson asked over his shoulder.

"The 201st Artillery," said Jack.

The road was empty until they caught up with a long line of trucks, Jeeps, and men on foot, all headed in the same direction. Sitting in the back of the truck with Charlie's head in his lap, Jack asked the GI next him, "Know where we're headed?"

"Mariveles. Case you don't know, Mariveles is the end of the line. You can't go no farther unless you're a damn good swimmer. And even then fucking sharks will get you."

Mariveles was a town on the southernmost tip of Bataan separated by a narrow stretch of water from the island fortress of Corregidor. At Mariveles they would make their stand and if they couldn't hold off the Japanese hoards then they would surely be boated to the island to await the promised reinforcements.

* * *

Lt. Kenji Tanaka's unit had been fighting nonstop for weeks. Looking down the road for any sign of the retreating Americans, he felt that maybe it would all be over soon. He didn't know how much more his men could take. Their losses had been heavy and many had battle wounds, fevers, and festering sores from fighting in the swamps and jungles of this miserable country.

The latest American retreat had been a mass panic, and they no longer made a pretext of trying to stop the Japanese advance. During the last few days, Kenji had passed through a sea of abandoned weapons, backpacks, canteens, and even pieces of clothing. Bodies of American soldiers black, swollen and covered with flies and maggots-lay everywhere

And the most telling sign of all that the Americans were a beaten force was that they were leaving behind their wounded. They sat or lay beside the road, too weak to go any farther. Dazed, defeated, demoralized men. Vacant stares which looked but saw nothing.

Kenji watched as several soldiers approached an American. His left foot was covered with a bloody bandage and he stood unsteadily with the aid of a crude crutch fashioned from a tree limb. As the American raised his right arm, in what Kenji thought was an attempt to surrender, a Japanese soldier fired a single shot into the man's abdomen. Startled disbelief came across the Americans face as he fell backwards into a sitting position, long legs splayed in front. The other Japanese soldiers laughed as the one who had fired the shot, walked to the fallen American and, with his foot, pushed the dying American into a muddy ditch.

"Why did you do that? He was trying to surrender!" Kenji shouted.

The man, who was not part of Kenji's unit, just laughed and said, "My Commander has told us that we can't take wounded prisoners; we don't have enough food or medicine."

"I can't believe any officer would give such an order. Have you never heard of The Geneva Convention? It doesn't allow you to kill a prisoner for such a reason.

It clearly calls for humane treatment for prisoners of war, including care for the sick and wounded."

Mocking Kenji with a short laugh, the soldier turned and walked away.

Kneeling, Kenji took a small packet of cards and papers from the dead American's pocket. Among the items was a picture of a pretty, young girl and a letter written in a neat feminine hand, which started "My Dearest Buster." Kenji lifted the two small metal pieces that hung from the neck.

Boyd E Bowles

3847586 T 41

O Pos

Protestant

* * *

As the convoy approached Mariveles, an MP directed them to turn down a side road that led to a large open area east of town. Jack thought it strange that they would set up defensive positions in an area so devoid of cover. No buildings or trees. No protection from the Japanese guns. After stopping, LeBeau and a few noncoms huddled with

Lt. Carson for several minutes and then returned to the truck where the men waited.

"We're gonna stop here while the lieutenant gets some kind of orders," LeBeau said.

The place where they had stopped was an airfield filled with thousands of American and Filipino troops as well as Filipino civilians. Many were wounded and sat or laid in the shade of vehicles. But mostly, they just stood idle waiting for someone to tell them what to do next.

Jack looked out over the vast throng and thought briefly about trying to find his unit, but knew it would be futile and sank slowly to the ground.

They had been at war for over four months and the constant fighting and lack of adequate rations had taken its toll and he just wanted to rest. In ways it seemed like a lifetime, but in other ways it seemed just yesterday that he'd seen the man cut down by the Japanese fighter in front of the PX.

Lt. Carson returned and gathered LeBeau and the other noncoms around him. Jack wasn't close enough to hear what was being said, but he could tell it probably wasn't good news. One turned and Jack saw that he was crying.

Another slammed his helmet to the ground and sent it rolling across the ground with a vicious kick.

When the group dispersed, Lt. Carson and LeBeau walked back and stood silently in front of the assembled men for several minutes before the lieutenant began to speak.

"I just got back from a meeting of commanders at Gen. King's command post. It has been decided that further resistance is impossible and we are to lay down our arms and surrender to the Japanese." The men were too stunned to speak; several began to weep. Lt. Carson continued. "I know how all of you feel and I feel the same way. We've fought our asses off, but we only have two days' worth of rations left and no meds for the sick and wounded. We're just about out of ammo and, if we keep fighting, General King thinks it will be a slaughter. He takes full responsibility for the surrender and directed that you be told that you have nothing to be ashamed of. You've fought the good fight and can always hold your head high."

"What does Gen. MacArthur say?" One man shouted from the rear of the group.

"He's been ordered to Australia so he can continue to lead the fight against the Japs. Before he left, he vowed he would return."

Another man spoke. "We've already heard that you might as well be dead as be a prisoner of the Japs." Another said, "Back up around Clark, I saw one of my buddies get a bayonet stuck in his gut when he tried to surrender."

Some of the men were talking among themselves, and another shouted, "I think we outta keep fighting."

"I know", said Carson. "I've heard the stories and seen some pretty bad things myself, but if you surrender there's a chance to survive. If you keep fighting, you'll surely die."

There was a murmur of agreement from some of the men, but the man who had said they should keep fighting spoke again. "Well, if I keep fighting, at least I can take some of those dirty sons-a-bitches with me."

"Everyone may not feel the same as you, Owens. If you're going to fight to the end, I suggest you go out and meet the Japs away from the ones that want to take their chances with surrender."

"What about Corregidor?" said another.

"There's no boats."

Jack couldn't believe what he was hearing. Anyone could have seen what was coming for weeks. Maybe Dick was right and there never had been any reinforcements coming. Maybe they had been written off and their lives were being sacrificed to buy time until the U.S. could recover from the surprise attacks.

Lt. Carson spoke again. "Any man who would like to try to escape is free to leave now. You may be able to reach the mountains where Filipino guerrilla fighters are still holed up, but you need to go now. The Japanese are very close."

Several men got up and started off towards the distant mountains. Jack knew Charlie didn't have the strength to reach the mountains. They had already come through a lot together and he wasn't going to leave him now. Surrender, as risky as it was, was their only chance. He wanted to believe that man would show compassion towards his fellow man-regardless of his nationality or skin color.

CHAPTER 9

The men pulled together into one large mass as they waited for the Japanese to arrive. The civilians tried to move to the center, as if somehow the soldiers could still protect them from the Japanese. Having none of the A Battery men around, Jack and Charlie stayed close to the group headed by Lt. Carson and Sgt. LeBeau. LeBeau, the "Raging Cajun," looked like he could take care of himself and lead his men through the worst of times. Jack's feeling about LeBeau was well founded. Born in New Orleans, the son of a prostitute who plied her trade in the French Quarter, LeBeau survived the mean streets by stealing from the outdoor markets, rolling drunks, and fighting the other boys who tried moving into his territory. He was small but tough and seldom lost a fight.

What weapons they had were stacked in the open. They knew their fighting, at least for now, was over and it would be dangerous to have a weapon when the Japanese arrived. Many sat with their heads hanging between their knees. If they talked at all, it was about everything except the war and the fate that awaited them.

Suddenly, men began to stand and look toward the road. Jack rose and saw a long line of Japanese trucks and tanks approaching. Japanese soldiers stood in the trucks, waving white flags with a solid red circle. Others were shouting and shaking clenched fists above their heads, while others fired guns in the air and aimed them menacingly at the huddled American and Filipino troops. Everyone stared in apprehension as the enemy soldiers leaped from the vehicles and swarmed over them like bees.

Jack stepped in front of Charlie when a Japanese soldier approached. Charlie's entire body shook from the fever that racked his body.

The Japanese soldier stopped in front of one of the other men, and saying something no one understood, pointed to the GI, then to himself, and putting two fingers to his lips drew in a deep breath. Jack knew he wanted a cigarette, but the American just stood there with a blank expression on his face until Owens, standing next to him, said, "The little monkey wants a cigarette."

The Japanese soldier whirled and smashed Owens across the mouth with his rifle butt. Owens crumpled to the ground, spewing blood and broken teeth. One of the men bent down to help Owens and was struck on the back of the head, opening a large gash in his skull. Others started to rush to the aid of their buddies but were restrained by those who understood the risk of any overt move.

The Japanese soldier turned and stared at the man who hastily withdrew a crumpled sweat stained, pack of Camels from his shirt pocket. The Japanese took out a cigarette, sniffed its aroma, then stuck it in his mouth, all the while staring at the American. After a pause, the American dug in his pocket and brought out a Zippo lighter and handed it to the Japanese. The Japanese lit his cigarette and then held up the Zippo, admiring its glint in the sun, before stuffing it and the cigarettes in his pocket.

Other Japanese circulated among the men, taking watches, rings, money, and dog tags. Even the photos of girlfriends and wives. They took anything of value except canteens and mess kits. One approached Jack and pointed to his high school ring. Because he had lost so much weight, the ring slipped off easily. After he had pocketed the ring, the Japanese motioned for Jack to empty his pockets. Jack turned them inside out to show there was nothing else. The soldier glared at him and Jack feared that somehow the Japanese could tell he was hiding the locket he had bought for Laura. He had wrapped it in a propaganda leaflet and stuffed it into the toe of his left shoe. For a tense moment, their gaze locked and then the Japanese soldier abruptly turned and walked away. This went on for the rest of the day. An occasional rifle shot would tell the frightened men another prisoner had been executed. It might be something as minor as moving too slow to obey a command...a command that couldn't even be understood. It might just be a wrong look on a man's face. It might be nothing at all.

When an officer walked by, Lt. Carson stepped out. "Sir, do you speak English?"

The Japanese officer stopped and looked Carson straight in the eyes.

"As well as you," he said in perfect English. "I went to UCLA. What is your name?"

"Lt. Carson."

"What do you want, Lt. Carson?"

"Sir, I wish to lodge a protest. The Geneva Convention requires that captured soldiers be treated with dignity and respect. I have seen men hit, brutally beaten and even shot without provocation."

"Lt. Carson, your country and mine have been at war for over four months. During that time, your soldiers have killed many fine, young Japanese men. That is all the provocation they need."

"But sir, we have surrendered. For these men, the war is over and they should not be treated in this barbaric manner."

The Japanese officer stepped so close that their faces were only inches apart. "We are not barbarians," he said in a quite steady voice. Then, still staring into Carson's eyes, he shouted something in Japanese and two soldiers grabbed Lt. Carson by the arms. Several Americans made a move to aid Carson but were shoved away by other Japanese soldiers. They watched helplessly as the lieutenant was dragged off. There was no doubt in Jack's mind that they would never see him again.

* * *

When Lt. Kenji Tanaka first saw the captured Americans and Filipinos gathered on the deserted airfield, he could hardly believe his eyes. There were literally tens of thousands of men, women and children as far as the eye could see. The soldiers, many in clothing so tattered it looked like they had been adorned with strips of *tanazaku* paper the people in Japan hung from their houses and trees during the *Tanabata* celebration, stood and watched the approaching Japanese convoy. Many had dirty bandages covering their wounds. As they drew closer, Kenji could see the vacant stares of men bewildered by defeat and couldn't help but think that these haggard, beaten men had once been part of a proud army.

"How can we handle this many prisoners?" He turned to Kochi. "I'm not sure we have enough food and medicine."

"That is not our worry, Kenji. You saw it yourself. They left tons of perfectly good food and medicines behind when they retreated. I have no sympathy for them."

"That's true, but now we must take care of them."

"I feel no obligation to take care of these dogs," Kochi voice rose. "Look at all of *our* soldiers they killed. How can you even care?"

Kenji's face flushed with anger, "What did you expect? They were soldiers fighting for their lives."

"Well, it doesn't really matter, does it?"

"What do you mean?"

"Just look for yourself. Most of them are half dead already. We couldn't save them if we tried."

Kenji shook his head. "But we *must* try."

* * *

Months of fighting, and near starvation had wrung the strength from their bodies like a twisted rag sheds its water. Demoralized, most of the prisoners had no thoughts about escaping. Never had so many American soldiers been defeated and captured at one time. Now they had neither the strength nor the will to do anything but follow the orders of their captors.

Jack lay so that Charlie could use his stomach as a pillow. During the night, Jack put his hand on Charlie's forehead. The fever had broken. Maybe they were in for some good luck for a change. Only then did he sleep.

Shouts from the Japanese guards awoke Jack with a start. The guards moved among the prisoners, prodding them to their feet with bayonet tipped rifles, and began separating them into groups of fifty men. Terrified civilians were separated from the soldiers and many began to cry, believing they were being separated so that they could be executed. Americans soldiers were separated from the Filipinos, and there was an attempt to separate enlisted from officers, but those with any rank showing ripped it off and threw it to the ground. Many, trying to stay with someone they knew, moved slowly or tried to withdraw further into the crowd, only to be slapped or kicked, or sometimes shot, by the guards. When a group was assembled, they were formed in columns on the road, Filipinos on the left, Americans on the right-and the march began.

No one knew where they were being taken or what fate awaited them but Jack was relieved that Charlie's fever had broken because he knew that they would require every once of strength they could muster.

When the guards came their way Jack and Charlie would melt further into the crowd and weren't selected to march that first day. No food or water for 24 hours was causing them to grow weaker by the hour. Many suffered from scurvy and beriberi. Nearly everyone had dysentery, and some, like Charlie, malaria. Jack was scared to think of what the future held. They had already seen examples of Japanese cruelty, but Jack tried to stay positive.

"Don't worry Charlie. When we get to a regular camp we'll get food and medicine."

As they awaited their fate, their spirits were lifted when they heard the big guns on Corregidor begin once more to roar, proving that there was still some fight left on their side. As long as the fight was still going on, there was hope they could still come out of this alive.

Darkness once again brought some relief from the unrelenting sun. The ground, once covered with grass, had been trampled into a barren surface as hard as concrete. Toilet facilities didn't exist, and the stench grew worse by the hour when the guards wouldn't allow them move away from the crowd to relieve themselves. Flies, attracted by the open sores, urine and feces, swarmed about their heads with a mind-torturing buzz. Jack had never spent a more miserable night in his life, and although the coming day would bring more uncertainty, he welcomed the sight of the morning sun.

A truck drove up and the men lined up for a small cup of rice, but it ran out before even half the men could get a small portion. When one man didn't move through the line fast enough, a Japanese guard knocked the cup from his hand, spilling the contents on the ground. The guards laughed uproariously when the man, in desperation, got down on his hands and knees and tried to scoop the rice back into his cup. A little later, a water truck came and dispensed foul smelling brown water that Jack thought must have been sucked up from some water buffalo wallow but they drank it eagerly, knowing you could only live a few days without water.

Watching a group of prisoners marching by, Jack's heart jumped when he spied Capt. Clark and Sgt. Malloy. A large bandage covered half of Capt. Clark's face and he walked with a slow, shuffling gait. Malloy's disheveled hair and tattered uniform was a far cry form the spit and polish top kick they had known but the erect walk, shoulders back, chin thrust forward...it was Samuel Malloy. Jack searched in vain for other members of A Battery, but there were none. Jack pointed out Clark and Malloy to Charlie.

"Wonder where the other guys are?"

"Maybe they got separated from the rest like we did," Jack replied.

"They could all be dead too."

They always taught new recruits how to act if taken prisoner of war. The NCO that had given the lecture said that according to The Geneva Convention all you ever had to tell the enemy was your name, rank and serial number. You didn't have to reveal your unit, where you were stationed or even the name of your hometown. It was your duty as a soldier in the United States Army to resist the enemy any way you could.

When Japanese soldiers with bayonets fixed to their rifles began yelling and making motions for groups to form columns on the road, Jack could see very few ways to resist. When a man moved slowly or acted like he didn't understand what was wanted of him, he risked being hit, shoved or even worse, bayoneted by a guard. It was obvious the NCO that gave the lecture had never been a POW, because even these small tokens of resistance brought vicious reactions from the Japanese. One of the men had been slow to follow orders, and a Japanese guard rammed his bayonet into his chest so hard that it went completely through him. As the man pitched backward, the rifle was jerked from the grasp of the Japanese soldier and the bayonet, protruding from the Americans back, stuck into the hard ground. The gun, butt pointing skyward, quivered with each beat of the heart until with one last terrible shudder, it stopped.

In this war, resisting would probably be your last act.

* * *

Early the next day, Jack and Charlie were prodded to their feet and were lined up on the road. The slight, deeply tanned Sgt. LeBeau, mistaken for a Filipino, was pushed protesting from the American side to the Filipino side and the columns started moving slowly north. There were only three or four guards for the entire group Jack was in and they strutted up and down the middle of the road between the columns like pompous marionettes, yelling *"hayaku"*, *"hayaku"*, *"hayaku."* The men soon learned that *"hayaku"* meant hurry. When a man wasn't walking fast enough, a guard would yell *"hayaku"* and strike him with the butt of his rifle or lunge in his direction with the point of a bayonet, coming within inches of the chest. Sometimes, seemingly only for sadistic pleasure, the guards would prod the column to move at a slow run until someone would drop from exhaustion. When someone fell, the guards would beat the fallen man senseless.

As they marched, rumors as to where they were being taken were whispered from man to man. The most frequent was that they were being taken to Clark Air Base where they would be exchanged for Japanese prisoners. Clark was a long way and Jack knew many of them wouldn't survive.

Walking under the hot sun was difficult, and fatigue struck even the strongest men; Jack devised a way to keep him and Charlie going. They would pick out a landmark ahead...a bend in the road, a stand of trees, the crest of a hill...anything to serve as a goal. When they reached that goal they would choose another. Jack knew that striving to reach each goal would keep them going and each torturous step would bring them closer to their destination.

They had walked just a few miles when a man ahead staggered into the center of the road, only to be pushed back in line by a guard. After a few more paces, he pitched face forward to the ground. Men walking behind the fallen man stopped and attempted to lift him but were forced by the guards to leave him where he fell. As Jack neared, the man raised himself to his hands and knees but didn't have the strength and sunk back to the ground, rolling over on his back. Jack paused, looking down into the man's stricken face.

"Come on, Jack," Charlie grabbed Jack's arm. "They'll kill you if you stop."

Jack jerked away from Charlie's grasp but before he could reach down, the man waved him away and said in a hoarse barely audible, whisper, "Go on. I ain't gonna make it anyway. No use anybody getting killed over me."

Jack moved off, looking back briefly, he watched the man try to rise and fall once again. Without warning, a shot rang out. An involuntary shudder ran through his body…he didn't need to look back to know what happened.

As the long, hot, day wore on without rest, food, or water, more men began to fall or just sit down. The Japanese guards shouted and kicked at the men. Those unable to keep going were summarily executed on the spot. When this happened, the others would draw on some inner strength to keep on for a while longer. Once when they came upon a muddy pool of black water, several men broke from the column, dropped flat on the ground, and began to suck the water into their parched mouths. The seemingly black water was really a solid mass of flies that rose and hovered above their the men's heads as they drank the putrid water, only to settle back down on the surface when the men were finished drinking. Jack thought that the men's' actions would surely bring the wrath of the guards down on them, but they just stood and laughed, knowing the men would be doubled over with cramps within the hour.

Jack thought they had marched at least ten miles when they stopped at the edge of a small village. The people brave enough to stay in their homes as the war swirled around them, stood at the side of the road and watched as the prisoners were herded into a open area. The hooves of cattle had turned the ground into a soft pulp but now the cattle were gone, probably slaughtered and eaten by the

Japanese army. At first, the Filipinos just stood and stared. Then a small boy went to a hut and came out with a bowl of rice and gave it to one of the men. The other Filipinos watched for the guards' reaction, and when the bravery of the young boy went unpunished, others began to bring loaves of bread, jugs of water, fruit, anything that could feed a famished man.

The soft, manure-laden field was the first good thing that had happened to the prisoners all day. The ground felt like a feather mattress compared with the field at Mariveles where the hard packed ground rubbed the skin raw. As they settled down, LeBeau, who had been separated from the Americans at the beginning of the march and forced to march on the Filipino side of the road, crawled over to where Jack and Charlie sat. In barely more than a whisper, he said, "This here is Manuel." LeBeau nodded toward a Filipino soldier who followed him. "Manuel and me has been doing a lot of talking while we was on our little walk today. We've been watching these Japs too and it wouldn't take a Houdini to get away from this bunch. Just a little step to the side, duck into the grass, and you're gone."

Charlie's face lit up. "You really think we could get away, Sarge?"

"Ain't no doubt in my mind."

"Even if you got away clean, where would you go?" Jack interjected. "The country's crawling with Japs...you'd be caught for sure."

LeBeau again nodded toward the dark man squatting behind him. "Manuel here is from the Zambales Mountains and he tells me that there's a bunch of headhunters up there who hate these fucking Japs. He'll lead us up there and we'd be safe till the war's over."

"Where the hell is the Zambales Mountains?" Jack asked.

"That way." This time, it was Manuel who spoke as he pointed to the north. " I take you there."

Jack stared at the little man. He was short and muscular with much darker skin than the average Filipino. Barefooted, he wore only a tattered pair of trousers, cut off at the knees. Was Manuel a headhunter, Jack wondered?

"I'm not sure I want to go live with a bunch of headhunters," Jack said.

"Only take heads of enemy," said Manuel. "You friend. Jap enemy. My people like Filipino and white people."

"What do you mean they like Filipinos? Aren't they Filipinos?"

"Not really." LeBeau answered for Manuel. "He told me all about them. They're called *Negritos*. They're the natives of these islands and still live like they did a thousand years ago. They're little people like Manuel here. They hunt with poison arrows and blow guns?" LeBeau chuckled. "Ain't that the shits. Blow guns and poison arrows in this day and time. Manuel says the little fuckers are the best hunters, trackers and fighters in the world."

"I don't know," said Jack.

"Well, I don't care if they're headhunters or a bunch of damn cannibals, I'm taking my chances with them. Anybody wants to come along is welcome."

"When are you going to try?" Jack asked.

"The sooner the better. I'd go tonight if I thought I could, but I think it would be better in the daytime when you can see where all the guards are. If I can see the bastards, I can get away."

"How far are we from these mountains you're talking about?" Jack asked.

"Best I can tell, 50, 60 kilometers at the most."

"Why not wait till we're closer?"

"Shit man, ain't you been watching what's going on around here?" asked LeBeau. "They must have killed a dozen guys today alone. Stay on this march, and you'll be lucky to last another day."

Silence came over the little group then LeBeau spoke again. "I'm going the first chance I get. I'll signal when it's time."

As LeBeau and Manuel crawled away, Jack and Charlie fell silent, lying back on the ground in an attempt to get some rest before the next grueling day began. From somewhere close, he heard a man groaning in obvious pain and occasionally someone would go into a coughing spasm that would last for several minutes. He could hear men talking in hushed tones, someone struggle to his feet to urinate, and then another faint sound…Jack couldn't quite make out what it was. It sounded like water gurgling slowly over rocks. Only when it stopped did he realize that he had been listening to a death rattle.

* * *

Lt. Kenji Tanaka was summoned to the abandoned hanger where Col. Kamura had set up his headquarters. The colonel was bent over a table intently studying a jumble of papers. When Kenji saluted and announced his presence, Col. Kamura looked up and then, without replying, returned his attention to the papers. Kenji stood waiting for his commander to turn his attention to him. After several minutes, Col. Kamura, finished with what he had been reading, straightened up and said, "Ah yes, Lt. Tanaka. We have been given responsibility for the prisoners and we must march them to the town of San Fernando. I'm assigning you to the detachment at San Fernando. You will be Capt. Aoki's second in command. Take a vehicle and driver and proceed to San Fernando, where you will assist Capt. Aoki in moving the prisoners through San Fernando. Facilities at San Fernando are extremely limited and the prisoners must be moved through as quickly as possible."

Col. Kamura turned back the table.

"Sir, may I say something?"

"Of course."

"Sir, it has been my observation that the enemy soldiers are in very poor condition. I don't believe many can survive a march of 100 kilometers."

"And what would you have us do?"

"Well sir, perhaps we could treat the wounded, provide more rations to the most undernourished, and transport the most severely sick and wounded to San Fernando by truck."

"Anything else?"

Kenji was afraid that he had already said too much, but had heard that the colonel was a fair and understanding man. Perhaps he really didn't know what was going on. "Sir, I have witnessed cruel and inhuman treatment of the prisoners."

Turning away, Col. Kamura clasped his hands behind his back. "What have you seen?"

"I have seen prisoners shot and bayoneted because they were slow to follow orders. I have seen them beaten for no reason, often in the presence of an officer with power to prevent it. In fact, I have seen officers themselves take part in this cruelty. I respectfully believe that prisoners of war should not be treated in this manner."

Col. Kamura wheeled quickly, his face contorted with anger. Pointing to the table strewn with papers, he said, "Lieutenant, do you know what those papers are?"

Before Kenji could reply. "Of course you don't, but for your information they are inventories of what rations we have left. Medical supplies. Food and fuel. Do you know what they show? They show that we don't have enough food and medicine for our own troops, much less *70,000* prisoners. And barely enough fuel to move our own troops, much less transport our sick and wounded enemy?"

Kenji knew there were great many prisoners, but not *that many.*

" I'm sorry sir. I now understand why food and medical care are difficult."

"Difficult is not the proper term, lieutenant. It is impossible."

Col. Kamura's tone softened. "Lieutenant, no one expected us to take this many prisoners and we're just not prepared. There is little we can do about it now."

"But that is no excuse for the brutal treatment I've seen," Kenji said.

Col. Kamura stepped closer to Kenji. "Lieutenant, have you ever had a pet...a dog or cat perhaps? And did you ever accidentally step on it's tail when it was lying in the way? And even though it wasn't the pet's fault, did you lash out at it in anger? That is the way people often react. Do you understand what I'm saying?"

Without waiting for an answer, Col. Kamura went on. "That is much like the situation here. Our enemy was poorly trained and equipped and because of their ineptness, we have been put in a very difficult position. We can't feed and care for them properly and that makes our men angry and in that anger they lash out at them. Can you understand that?"

Kenji understood what the colonel was saying, but there was a great deal of difference between stepping on a pet's tail, and ramming a bayonet through a man. He thought of saying so but realized that any further protest would not only be futile but foolish as well. Instead he said, "Yes sir, I understand."

CHAPTER 10

Jack awoke with a start unable to remember where he was. Who were these men lying all around? As he rubbed his eyes, it started to come back to him. The first days march. The unrelenting heat. The cruelty of their captors. He, like the others was in the most desperate of situations. He was the prisoner of a vicious enemy who had as little regard for human life as anyone could imagine, being marched to an unknown fate, through a sun that could fry a man's brain, and with only the barest amount of food and water to sustain life. He didn't know how or when it would end but he knew that for better or worse it would someday end. Maybe, just maybe, some angel would watch over him, and make sure he got out of this alive.

As the sun slowly climbed above the horizon, Japanese guards strode through the lot yelling, kicking, and prodding with their bayonets to get the men on their feet. Jack saw a man fail to respond to repeated kicks and he was sure this was the man whom he had heard gasp his last breath the night before.

The morning ratio of rice arrived in the back of an olive drab truck marked "U.S. Army" with a white star on its door.

Sgt. LeBeau edged up beside Jack. "See that bullet hole right there in the star? Shit man that's our truck. A Jap bullet came right through that door and shaved Chandlers belt buckle off. Don't that just burn your ass? Using our truck to haul around their shitty rice."

As they had retreated into Bataan, orders to destroy their equipment had been given, but much had been captured by the enemy. It made him wonder how many American soldiers were killed with their own guns and bullets.

The men barely had time to finish their rice before the guards shouted at them to move out. Passing through the next village, they saw a free-flowing water well at the side of the road. Crazed with thirst, several of the men broke from the column and draped over the concrete wall, filling their canteens and gulping mouthfuls of the precious life saving water. Unsure of how the guards would react, the other's stood and watched. A guard watched five men get a drink and fill their canteens. Then, without warning, he shot one of the men through the head. The man's body slumped over the side of the well as blood clouded the clear sparkling water. The guards pointed and laughed as the other men at the well turned and ran back to the line of marching men.

This latest display of wanton disregard for a human life affected the prisoners more than any thing they had witnessed so far. Now all of the prisoners had the look of abject fear that desperate men get when facing almost certain death and they all had the same thoughts...*Am I next? What must I do to stay alive?*

The road, built to handle light vehicles, became increasingly difficult to walk on. The heavy trucks, tanks, and impacting artillery shells had chewed it up like a giant jackhammer. Large chunks had been gouged from the soft asphalt, and holes large enough to swallow a jeep made the going difficult.

A man Jack knew to be a colonel stepped into a hole and twisted his ankle so severely he could barely walk. The men around him were afraid to help, not knowing if their captors would permit it, and the colonel fell further and further back in the column. Jack knew when the last man passed the injured man would probably be shot. Jack could count at least 5 men who had been killed for the same reason.

"Charlie, we have to help him."

"Think they'll let us?"

"We can't just let him die without trying."

Positioning themselves on each side of the crippled man and pulling his arms over their shoulders, they labored to keep up with the column. The guards gave them menacing stares but made no move to interfere.

As they tired, Jack turned to some of the nearby men. "Can you guys give us a hand here?" The men walked silently on. The natural instinct to survive had taken over and none were willing to risk their lives to save another. Finally unable to go further, they stopped and eased the crippled man into a sitting position. As the last of the column passed, the colonel, saw a Japanese guard staring at them. Reaching inside his shirt, he pulled out a limp, sweat-stained piece of paper, and pressed it into Jack's hand.

"That has my wife's name and address on it. Try to remember it, and if you get out of this alive, give her my love and tell her how I died. Now you fellows go on. You can't help me anymore."

Jack and Charlie hesitated. "That's an order."

Jack quickly stuffed the paper into his pocket. He knew they were under the watchful eye of one of the more tolerant guards, but he knew a guard's mood could change in seconds. As he and Charlie hurried to catch up, he looked back at the colonel, who raised his right hand in salute. Jack drew his body to attention and, with his eyes misting over, returned the honor.

* * *

Kenji had been on the road only a short time when his vehicle overtook the first group of prisoners marching north. He wondered how this sorry looking group could still be walking, much less make to San Fernando. He was moved by their condition, but they were the enemy. And they *did* have to be moved to San Fernando. That was the only way they could get to permanent camps where he was sure they could be properly fed and cared for. Then he saw something that disturbed him even more...an increasing number of corpses lay on the side of the road, some covered with flies bloating and turning black under the hot tropical sun. Many were battle casualties and had been dead for several days. Others, however, looked as if they had been dead only a short time. Kenji wanted to believe that these men had died of their wounds or sicknesses, but when he passed one lying in a pool of fresh blood, the head severed from his body, he knew it could only have been done by the blade of an officer's sword. Trying to rationalize the man's execution Kenji could think of nothing that would warrant that kind of response from one of his fellow officers.

After seeing the headless corpse, Kenji kept his eyes glued to the road ahead, trying to ignore the bodies they passed. Watching the road ahead, he saw a convoy of four trucks approaching, still moving troops south for the continuing battle to capture Corrigedor.

The road was only about 20 feet wide. As his driver pulled to the side to let the larger trucks pass, Kenji saw another dead American soldier lying in the middle of the road. He lay on his back and his moment of death had frozen him with one hand raised and a finger pointing skyward as if he were trying to indicate to whoever took his life that his God was watching. As the lead truck approached, Kenji expected it to veer around the lifeless form. Instead, it ran directly over the body with a bounce of its large wheel. As the truck roared past, Kenji saw the two soldiers in the cab laughing as if running over the dead American was a hilarious joke. To his horror, the second truck in the convoy also drove directly over the mangled corpse. Kenji closed his eyes so that he wouldn't see if the third and fourth trucks ran over the body. When he finally looked, he saw only a mangled mass of flesh and bone. The only thing to suggest that this carrion in the road had ever been a living, breathing, human was a leg from the knee down, a worn, tattered shoe still on the foot. It had been ripped from the body and hurdled aside like a worn-out wooden leg.

* * *

The sun was directly overhead when the weary prisoners were allowed their first rest. They sat alongside the road, bordered on both sides by tall elephant grass. On the opposite side of the road, LeBeau, sitting beside Manuel, looked over, and made a slight movement of his head toward the high grass. Jack knew LeBeau's escape plan was about to be put into motion and the gritty little sergeant was inviting them to come along.

Jack and Charlie looked at each other. "What do you say, Jack? Do we go?"

"I don't think there's any way in hell they can make it."

"Me neither."

The Japanese guard nearest LeBeau turned and started walking toward the front of the column. With one last look, LeBeau and Manuel, in a crouching run, quickly covered the few feet to the wall of grass and disappeared. Jack watched for any reaction from the guards, but there was none. They had gotten past the first hurdle. Unless the Japanese guards could remember all of the prisoner's faces, and would know someone was missing, the two were well on their way to the Zambales Mountains. For a moment Jack regretted their not trying, but they would have had to go into the grass from the opposite side of the road, risking separation from LeBeau and Manuel. Without Manuel and his knowledge of the country, their chance for survival would have been poor.

The brief rest didn't include food or water and the prisoners were soon shouted, kicked, and prodded to their feet again. It seemed to infuriate the Japanese soldiers when their orders weren't understood by the Americans and Jack wondered if they thought all Americans could understand Japanese.

The group of guards they were under now included one they had already seen. He was a particularly brutal individual who'd shot two men the day before. He was aptly nicknamed "The Toad" because of his short, broad body and bowed legs. His oversized, shaved head seemed to grow directly from his shoulders and his body rolled from side to side as he walked. Men who showed a weakness were the savage guards specialty, and much like a lion would single out the young, wounded, or crippled prey, he would single out the lame, sick, or frightened prisoner for his malevolent attacks. Jack wondered what kind of a person the man was before a gun was placed in his hands and he was given the power of life or death over another human being. Did he amuse himself by tearing the legs off of bugs so that he could watch them squirm? Did he douse cats with gasoline, light it, and then watch their frenzied, fiery run until they collapsed in a charred mass of fur? Probably not. More than likely, he was like other men...he changed completely when given unrestricted power. And now he was a vicious killer. Jack and Charlie were careful not to attract his attention and as tired, hungry, and dehydrated as they were, they called on some inner strength to walk with their heads up and not waiver, stumble, or fall when The Toad was watching.

CHAPTER 11

It took Lt. Kenji Tanaka-the newly assigned second in command of the POW holding compound at San Fernando-eight hours to travel the 100 kilometers to San Fernando. His progress had been slowed by the constant need to pull to one side and stop when the big trucks rumbled by. The groups of prisoners had started the march at intervals, but now it was a steady stream of men. Many walked as if in a trance and, despite the sound of the engine and the blaring horn, were completely unaware when a truck was just behind them. The guards would push the prisoners aside and once Kenji watched as a guard struck a man in the head with his rifle butt. The man fell, blood flowing from his shattered skull. As his driver swerved around the unconscious man, Kenji could see the man was still alive but would require medical attention to survive. Medical attention he would never receive.

* * *

It was almost dark when the next day's march was called to a halt. It was an area of sparse trees and a single strand of barbed wire was strung from tree to tree to form a makeshift compound. Although it would have been a simple matter to step over the wire after darkness fell the bone weary prisoners gave little thought to escaping. The Japanese, knowing this, posted no guards at night. Shortly after the sun had set, several guards went into a thatched roofed house across the road from the compound. They entered with their customary shouting, and like quail flushed from the brush, an elderly couple fled out the door, faces contorted with fear. Then laughter and a sound that made Jack's skin crawl...a high-pitched female scream. The laughter and loud talk, punctuated with screams, continued well into the night, but, as time went on, the screams grew fainter until they stopped altogether. Occasionally, a drunken Japanese soldier would stagger out the door, urinate, and stagger back in.

Charlie sat with his arms resting on his drawn up knees, staring intently at the house. "Someday, these sons-a-bitches are gonna pay for this."

"Yeah, if there's any justice in the world, they will," said Jack. Then he added. "This shouldn't surprise us any. We've already seen them murder a bunch of people. Men that'll murder people in cold blood won't think twice about raping a woman."

It was hard to sleep, listening to the drunken orgy across the road, and Jack was relieved when the noise ended. He wondered if the outrage had ended because all of the drunken Japanese had finally passed out or because the girl had died.

The next morning there was no sign of life from the house and the guards were more surly and brutish than ever. They constantly jabbed prisoners with bayonets to make them walk faster and knocked several men to the ground with their rifle butts. As the sun climbed in the cloudless sky, they passed through a small village and the inhabitants lined the sides of the road, shouting encouragement to the American and Filipino prisoners. The infuriated guards tried to drive them away and when the people began throwing loaves of bread and fruit to the prisoners, the guards fired into the crowd. Several villagers, including a small girl, fell dead.

When the guards changed at noon, the prisoners rested briefly but received no food for the day. When the march resumed, Jack noticed the prisoners ahead looking and pointing off to the side of the road. As Jack drew near, he could see a man's lifeless body lashed to a tree, head sagging to the side, the chin almost touching the shoulder. As he got closer, he could see that the man was covered with stab wounds. His stomach had been ripped open and his intestines bulged through the wound. Big black flies swarmed around the body, fighting for a place to land. Suddenly Charlie stiffened, cried out, "*Malloy.*"

A Japanese guard whirled around at the sound.

"Damn it, Charlie, just keep walking," Jack said through clenched teeth.

"Why'd they have to that? The dirty bastards. Why'd they have to do that? The dirty bastards." Nothing could have prepared Jack for the sight of Master Sergeant Samuel Malloy bound to a tree and butchered. He was certain that Malloy hadn't died easily and had defied the Japanese until his last breath.

The following days were a blur. Seeing Malloy had taken a terrible toll. Jack's mind and body were numb. At times he felt that he'd left his body and was looking down on the ghastly scene from above. He could see the long column of men moving down the road, but there were no guards. He would shout down at them, telling them to run because the guards were gone. But when they looked up at him, there were black holes where eyes should have been and he knew they were all dead. And then a shout, a push, a stumble and he would be back on earth among the walking dead.

He no longer tried to set goals to keep them going. When a shot rang out, he hardly looked up. When a man fell by the side, he no longer worried that the man would be executed. His hope for survival was destroyed. Malloy was tough and strong. If they could kill Malloy, they could kill anyone.

* * *

Capt. Aoki was a short, broad-shouldered, stern-faced individual with a completely shaved head and chest full of campaign ribbons from combat duty in China. Sitting at a desk in the depot office, his baldhead glistening in the glare of the bare light bulb, he glared up at Kenji.

Standing at attention, Kenji saluted. "Lt. Tanaka reporting for duty."

"I received a call from Col. Kamura that you were coming."

"Sir, it will be my pleasure to serve under your command," Kenji said.

With a noticeable limp Capt. Aoki came around in front of the desk and stood directly in front of Kenji.

Looking up into Kenji's face he said through clenched teeth, "Really? Well, I must tell you that it is not my pleasure to be here, Lt. Tanaka. In fact, I hate it here. I'm a combat officer. I served in three different campaigns in China and Manchuria. The limp you see is the result of wounds I received in China. I shed blood for the glory of the Imperial Army and now I'm relegated to this cesspool of a place to load a bunch of American dogs on trains."

Kenji could see Capt. Aoki's jaw muscles working and could only stand in awkward silence at this display of bitterness from his new superior.

The captain's anger subsided, just as suddenly as it had erupted. Stepping back slightly, he placed his palms together and with a slight bow said, "Forgive me. That I'm here is not your fault."

"I understand your frustration, sir."

But the truth was that Kenji could not understand the captain's frustration at all. How could any man relish killing other men? Not that he was afraid of being wounded or killed. He had heard bullets buzzing like angry bees as he charged across the beaches of Luzon. At Cabanatuan he had felt the rush of adrenaline and the exhilaration that every man gets when exposed to danger. He knew that was part of being a soldier and he never felt fear until it was all over. He knew that his way of thinking was not in keeping with the *Samurai* spirit taught at the Academy. In the beginning he had that quality, but that all ended when he saw a man's head explode in a red shower of blood and brains. Now he would never understand why some men choose war over peace.

CHAPTER 12

Not till they entered San Fernando did the sight of Malloy begin to fade. Jack would never get over it, but he knew had to go on. By now, the column of prisoners had formed into one gigantic mass, forcing the guards to relax their rigid rules. The prisoners were allowed to walk in groups and talk freely among themselves.

Jack and Charlie talked about the fate of Capt. Clark. They wondered whether he could survive without the help of Malloy. They wondered why Malloy had been killed in such a vicious manner. They talked about their other friends...Buster, Dick, Enos, and Bobby and whether they would ever see them again. Regaining some optimism, Jack talked of what he would do when the war was over. Occasionally when they were allowed a brief rest, and no guard was near, he would slip the paper from his boot and read the name and address scrawled on it over and over. He would tell the colonel's wife about her husband's courageous death. The paper was torn and the ink had faded, but he could still read it...*Peggy Scanlon. 4306 Hartford St. Chicago, Il.* The paper and Laura's locket, still wrapped in the propaganda leaflet, were the only things of any value he still possessed.

* * *

Kenji spent his first few days in San Fernando preparing for the arrival of the first group of prisoners.

Moving 70,000 prisoners through San Fernando would be a monumental task and all they had was one ancient, wood-burning locomotive and six small, decrepit boxcars that had been built in 1918. Knowing prisoners would have to be held at least overnight awaiting transportation to Capas, Kenji readied several small warehouses. When Capt. Aoki learned Kenji was using their small contingent of men to clean the buildings, he became enraged and ordered it to stop. The boxcars that would be used to transport the prisoners had been used for livestock, and the floors were covered with manure and hay. When Kenji attempted to clean them Capt. Aoki once again ordered the men to stop and directed them to less meaningful tasks. To Kenji, it seemed the captain was doing everything he could to make their task, as well as the life of the prisoners, as difficult as possible.

* * *

The prisoners snaked their way through San Fernando and, as they approached the city's center, Jack saw a train belching black smoke, pulling away from the depot, all of its doors closed except one. As it moved by Jack could see a man's gaunt face through the narrow opening. In the tropical heat, the boxcars would be like ovens. Jack figured the men would be lucky to survive even the briefest trip.

As they rested beside the tracks, rumors spread that they would be exchanged for Japanese prisoners. "Man, you guys ain't learned much about these damn Japs," Charlie scoffed. Didn't you see these bastards in battle? There ain't no Jap prisoners. They keep fighting 'till you have to kill 'em. Or else they do that "hairy carry" shit. Either way, there ain't no damn Jap prisoners to trade for."

Charlie wasn't the most eloquent person Jack had ever heard, but what he said usually made sense. Several men gave Charlie angry looks, as if he'd just stolen something valuable from them. In fact, he had...he had stolen their hope.

They had been sitting in the hot sun for several hours when a tall Japanese officer came out of the depot and said something to the guards. The guards immediately began gesturing for the men to rise and move to a dilapidated warehouse down the tracks. Guards pulled open the large, double doors revealing a dark interior with a single shaft of sunlight filtering through a small hole in the corrugated tin roof. It would be the first time they had been sheltered from the sun and the afternoon rains, which came at the same time everyday. The rains washed away the dust and offered a brief respite from the heat. The men would cup their hands attempting to catch a bit of the precious fluid and hold open mouths skyward like a new born bird to wet their dry mouths. However, when the rains ended the humidity would soar, making the heat all the more unbearable. What little water they could glean from the rains would soon be sucked from their bodies like a leech sucking blood.

* * *

Kenji Tanaka watched as the prisoners entered. A meticulous planner, he had measured the warehouse and, allowing one square meter for each man, had figured that 200 prisoners could be placed inside. Counting off 200 men, Kenji blocked the way of the next man in the column, an American much shorter than himself. Walking with his eyes on the ground, the prisoner almost bumped into Kenji before realizing that he wouldn't be allowed inside.

Startled, he cried out, *"Jack!"*

A tall American who had been the last man through the door rushed back out. Struck sharply across the chest with the butt of a guard's rifle, the man fell to the ground and the soldier lunged forward with his bayonet aimed squarely at the chest. Kenji reached out and deflected the bayonet, causing it to drive into the American's left shoulder. The American writhed in pain and, as he rolled over, Kenji saw a patch on his sleeve...an artillery gun pointed skyward, with the inscription *"201st"* stitched in red below the gun. The shorter man dropped to his knees and tore open the wounded Americans sleeve. Then, ripping off a piece of his own shirt, he gently wiped the blood away, revealing a beautiful red, white, and blue tattoo of an eagle, wings spread, clutching a bundle of arrows in it's talons. He looked into the wounded American's face and for a brief moment, their eyes locked. Kenji thought he saw a look of understanding.

* * *

Jack lay stunned as Charlie tried to stem the flow of blood. Slowly it came back to him. He had heard Charlie call his name and when he looked back, he saw the tall

Japanese officer blocking Charlie's path. It had become an obsession with him that he be Charlie's protector and see him through this thing alive. When he saw that they were being separated, he turned and, rushed back out the warehouse door. The next thing he knew, he was on his back staring into the murderous eyes of a Japanese soldier. As the soldier thrust the bayonet at his chest, the tall officer hand deflected the lethal blade. As Charlie knelt and tore away the sleeve, Jack stared up at the Japanese officer towering over him. He was the tallest Japanese he had ever seen and he looked more western than Japanese. Their eyes met and, for the first time since his capture, Jack saw genuine compassion and he was certain of one thing ...*the Japanese officer had saved his life.*

* * *

As Kenji and the soldier stood glaring at each other, Capt. Aoki shouldered through the prisoners gathered around the door.

"Lt. Tanaka, why have you stopped moving the prisoners into the building?"

"Captain, the building is full."

"Nonsense." Capt. Aoki peered into the dark interior. "There's room for many more. Move them in immediately."

Kenji nodded to the soldiers and they began to prod more prisoners inside. The wounded American struggled to his feet with the help of his smaller friend and moved past Kenji. Finally, when no more could possibly go in, Capt. Aoki ordered the doors closed and locked.

* * *

Charlie supported Jack as they moved into the warehouse. The prisoners pushed and elbowed each other in an attempt to gain a little space. Charlie worked toward the nearest wall where he believed the press of the prisoners would be less. Men grumbled and pushed back as Charlie forced their way through the crowd and Jack winced each time someone jostled his throbbing shoulder. When they reached the wall, Jack sank to the floor and lowered his head onto his drawn-up knees.

After the doors closed, the prisoners began to settle down, some sitting with their backs against each other for support and many, in an attempt to find sleep in the cramped space, curled into a fetal position. Charlie, with Jack's head resting on his shoulder, sat with his back against the wall. Each time he began to doze, Jack woke with a start and grabbed his injured shoulder. He had come perilously close to death and the vision of the bayonet being thrust at his chest flashed through his mind over and over. Each time it did, he willed himself instead to see the Japanese officer who had saved him. It was a face he would never forget.

As the night wore on, the oppressive sounds and smells within the warehouse settled over the prisoners. Sick and wounded moaned and cried for help that no one could give. Another man could be heard softly weeping. Nearby, Jack could hear someone muttering the 23rd Psalm over and over, *"Yea, though I walk through the valley of the shadow of death, I will fear no evil, for thou art with me."* That had been his Grandmothers favorite Bible verse and helped sustain her during his grandfather's long illness. Jack, in a barely audible whisper, joined in the prayer. ..."*though I walk through the valley of the shadow of death...*"

Night sometimes bought some relief from the heat but the closely packed bodies in the warehouse caused the temperature to soar. Men gasped as the malodorous air choked their lungs. But through it all, Jack was able to maintain his courage and sanity by repeating softly, *"Yea though I walk through the valley of the shadow of death, I will fear no evil for thou art with me, thy rod and thy staff they comfort me."*

Charlie suffered a malaria attack during the night, shaking so badly that his teeth chattered, but as the first rays of light came through the hole in the roof, his shaking stopped; his face felt cold and clammy to Jack's touch. He grasped his wrist, frantically searching for a pulse.

Charlie raised his head. "What's wrong"

"I thought you were dead. You've been burning up with fever and shaking all night."

"Maybe this goddamn oven sweated all the poison outta me."

The doors were thrown open at dawn and the men stumbled out, filling their lungs with the fresh morning air. Jack's shoulder still throbbed, but the arm no longer felt like a dead weight. He looked around for the tall Japanese officer who had saved his life. When he couldn't see him, an inexplicable panic swept over him. Maybe it had never happened. Maybe there was no tall Japanese officer. Maybe it had all been a dream in his feverish mind. It had become terribly important to be saved by his enemy. After seeing so much cruelty he needed an act of kindness to renew his faith in man's basic goodness.

"Charlie, do you see the one who pushed the bayonet away?"

Charlie rose on his toes and looking around, said, "No, I can't see him anywhere, but here comes that son of a bitch who packed us in last night."

The short, bald officer was limping toward the warehouse followed by several soldiers. Apprehensive that they would be forced back inside, the prisoners stood quietly and watched as the group disappeared into the dark interior. Moments later, the officer and his entourage reappeared, separated a group of prisoners, and ordered them back inside. The others shrank back from the entrance.

"They can kill me if they want, but I ain't going back in that shit hole," Charlie said, voicing a feeling most of them shared.

Then the Americans who had reentered came out carrying the bodies of dead Americans. One after another, the bodies were carried out until 22 men-who had succumbed to the heat-were lying on the ground. Guards thrust shovels into the hands of the nearest prisoners, who then began the task of burying their comrades in the black Philippine earth.

* * *

Kenji sat at a small desk in the depot working on supply requisitions and could see only a small portion of the prisoners standing outside the warehouse. Because of his reluctance to crowd more prisoners into the warehouse the previous day, he had been banished to administrative duties. Looking out the small window, he saw the soldiers go to the shed and return with the shovels. That could only mean that some of the prisoners had died during the night and must now be buried.

Capt. Aoki had not reprimanded him in front of the enlisted men at the warehouse, but had waited until they were back in the captain's office. Kenji had stood at attention while the captain limped back and forth ranting about everything his warped mind could think of...the quality of the young officers, the country's inept leaders, the despicable, cowardly Americans. Before the tirade ended, the captain had called everything about Kenji into question... his loyalty to his country, his courage, his ancestry...even his manhood. But the part that really bothered Kenji was when Capt. Aoki had questioned his loyalty to Japan. He loved his country and would gladly die on the battlefield-or anywhere else for that matter-if the cause were just. But a dirty warehouse in San Fernando wasn't the battlefield and he would not kill or permit to be killed, a defenseless man. Kenji knew he was serving his country better than Capt. Aoki, or the soldier who had shot the wounded, unarmed American on the road, because he knew that without morality, the country would surely wither and die.

Capt. Aoki had concluded. "You, Lieutenant Tanaka, are a disgrace to your country and the Imperial Army." Stopping directly in front of Kenji. "I could have you shot for aiding the enemy. Do you understand that?"

"Yes Sir."

"Can you explain your treasonous actions?"

He could but he didn't. If he said any of the things on his mind, it would only make matters worse.

So he simply answered, "No, Sir."

* * *

Jack and Charlie watched as four prisoners labored to dig the mass grave in the hard ground. The men, weakened by weeks of too little food and water, worked slowly. When one man sunk to his knees, a guard clubbed him in the head with his rifle butt. A low murmur swept through the prisoners, causing the guards to level their rifles at them as a warning. The prisoners could easily have rushed the 15 guards and overcome them, but many would have been killed in the effort. And then what? There was no place to hide. They would be tracked down and shot before the sun had set. So they did the only thing they could...stand and watch and silently curse the Japs.

Another prisoner was shoved into the shallow hole and directed to pick up the shovel of the fallen man. When two other prisoners tried to drag the fallen man out, the guards forced them back and he was left lying where he fell, blood oozing from his head.

Leaning close to Jack, Charlie said, "They're going to bury him and I don't think he's dead."

A big, blond man called "Swede" said loudly enough to cause a guard to look sharply in their direction, "If I see him move, I'm going in there after him."

Swede was almost as big as Sgt. Malloy had been and still looked like he could hold his own against anyone, but Jack knew it would be futile for anyone to go to the aid of the man lying in the unfinished grave.

"Don't be crazy, Swede," Jack said through clenched teeth. "There'll be two of you dead instead of one".

"I don't care no more."

"For Christ's sake, Swede," said Charlie, "keep your damn voice down. Get your ass killed if you want to, but I ain't ready to go just yet."

When the bald officer was satisfied with the depth and size of the grave, the guards ordered other prisoners to drag in the bodies while others covered them. The first shovels of dirt were purposely aimed to fall between the bodies, as if each man was loath to actually start the burying process. The Japanese guards, aware of what the men were doing, scurried around them shouting angrily. When dirt landed on the legs of the man who'd had been hit by the guard, Jack saw the man's arm move. Looking around at Swede, he could tell the big man had also seen it. Swede's hands were clenched in front of his chest and his teeth were clamped together so tight that Jack could see the jaw muscles quivering.

"Don't do it, Swede," Jack said softly. "Don't do it." And then louder so that he was sure Swede heard, "Maybe it was just a muscle contracting. That happens when people die." But Jack knew they were going to bury the man alive.

Swede said nothing but continued to stare intently at the grave. The shoveling continued until dirt hit the face of the still-alive man and he suddenly raised his head. The sight so unnerved Jack that a shudder went through his body and the skin on the back of his neck crawled.

The men with the shovels froze, and even the guards fell silent as they all watched the macabre scene...everyone except Swede. With a sound starting deep down in his belly and rising to a blood-curdling scream, Swede bolted toward the open grave. The first bullet struck him in the left side, but did nothing to slow him. The second bullet tore into his abdomen. The big man hesitated, shook his broad shoulders like a bull trying to shed the darts of the *banderillero*, and then continued his run. Jumping into the pit, Swede scooped up the man and leaped up to the grave's edge. Two more bullets slammed into Swede's chest before he, still clutching the body, fell back into the grave.

CHAPTER 13

As they were being loaded into the boxcars, Jack once again looked around for the tall Japanese officer who had saved his life. When he was in the car and could see over the heads of the other prisoners, he finally saw him standing in the doorway of the train depot. Jack was struck once again by his height. Jack was 6' 3" and he judged the Japanese officer to be at least that tall. He couldn't be sure, but he thought the officer was looking right at him. Then he saw an almost imperceptible nod of recognition.

* * *

Lt. Kenji Tanaka tried to keep a low profile after the incident at the warehouse door. He had heard shots but when he went to the window, he couldn't see past the throng of prisoners. The shots could only mean more prisoners had died. Later, as they were being loaded onto the train, he saw him again...the tall American with the bloody shoulder. The prisoner had paused in the boxcar door and looked directly at him. Kenji made a slight nod in the Americans direction and was sure he saw the man stand a little straighter as a look of recognition flashed across his face.

More prisoners arrived every day and were put on the trains for transport to Camp O'Donnell as quickly as possible but many died from illness or injuries before they could be moved out. But now Kenji stayed at his desk, trying to shut out what was going on around him and it was a relief when Capt. Aoki informed him that he would be reassigned to a combat unit. He might die in combat but at least he wouldn't be guilty of killing defenseless men.

* * *

Each small boxcar would hold 25 men comfortably but the Japanese forced over a 100 in each one. Without room to sit, they were forced to stand pressed tightly together. To those in the center it seemed as if all oxygen was being sucked from the air before it got to them. Many struggling to breathe pushed at those around them in an effort to get more air. The effect was like a row of dominos falling against each other. Men, in a jumble of bodies and limbs, fell on top of one another until the surge made its way all the way across the car only to stop when it pinned those on the edge against the wall. Jack and Charlie, among the last to climb on managed to stay near the boxcar door, breathing in whatever fresh air seeped through the loose-fitting door. When the train was fully underway the door was pushed open to allowing a rush of fresh air to sweep through the crowded space. As many as possible squeezed into the opening and sat dangling their legs out of the car.

Soon they passed the twisted and blackened ruins of the hangers and buildings of Clark Field. It was a depressing sight and they stared in silence at the utter destruction of what had been, before the war, the main U. S. military installation in the Philippines Islands. It was here that General MacArthur had made his headquarters and the main force of combat aircraft was stationed. Now, nothing was left. It was as if the Japanese had used Clark Field to symbolize their complete dominance over the Americans. Soon, all talk stopped and the prisoners sat silently listening to the click of the wheels and the creaking of the ancient boxcar as it rocked back and forth on the uneven tracks.

As the ruins of Clark Field faded, the tracks entered a thick jungle where Jack could see no more than a few feet into its dark interior.

As they crawled along, scarcely faster than a man could walk, one man, standing near the door gazed out and said, "Boys, this maybe the best chance we'll ever have to get away." He looked around for reaction from the other men, but saw only doubt on their faces.

"Is everybody here too much of a coward to make a run for it?" Again, no response.

"OK, I guess I'll go alone, and by God, I'll be back home sitting on my porch while you sons a bitches are rotting in some stink hole." With that e threw back his head and let out a high pitched laugh.

One of the other men said, "Don't be crazy Jim. You can't live two days in that jungle."

Without another word, Jim stepped between two of the sitting men and jumped. Jack leaned out the door and looked back. All he saw was the dense jungle closing in on the tracks behind them. Jim had been swallowed by the dense growth as if he had never existed.

Watching the desperate leap for freedom made Jack think of LeBeau. Maybe LeBeau had made it to The Zambales Mountains and at this very moment was sitting around a campfire with a bunch of headhunters. The tough little Cajun had something Jim didn't. He had a plan. You had to have a plan.

As the jungle began to thin, they passed scattered groups of Filipino's standing alongside the tracks. Some waved and shouted and at first Jack couldn't understand what they were saying. As he strained to hear, the words became clear. "GI" "GI," "GI."

As they went through a small village, Filipino boys ran alongside throwing bananas, balls of rice wrapped in banana leaves, pieces of cooked chicken, and mangos through the open door. Others handed up gourds of cool, clear water that were eagerly passed among the parched mouths until emptied and thrown back out to the boys running beside the train.

The scene was repeated in several small villages, but when they moved through a larger town, soldiers stood at the road crossings, keeping the Filipinos away from the tracks. At one crossing, Japanese soldiers struck the men who were sitting in the doorway across their feet and legs with long bamboo sticks. As they attempted to get their legs back inside, a soldier pushed the heavy door closed, pinning one man's leg just below the knee. As he struggled to free his leg, the Japanese continued to beat it with the bamboo sticks. He was finally able to get his leg in but not before his shoeless foot had been severely beaten.

Jack bent over the man. "It'll be OK. We'll get your foot wrapped up and it'll be OK."

The man looked at Jack and shook his head, "I appreciate what you're trying to do, but I'm a dead man."

"No. You'll have a sore foot, that's all." The other men who were peering at the bloody foot nodded their agreement.

Again the man shook his head. "They might as well have put a bullet in my brain. When we get off this train and I can't keep up, that's what they'll do. Put a bullet in my brain."

Jack knew what the man said was true.

Late in the afternoon, the train slowed as it passed a railroad sign painted with the word *Capas* in black letters. When they came to a complete stop, Japanese soldiers lining the the track motioned for the prisoners to come out of the car. Those with any strength left helped the weaker ones down. The man with the injured foot was lowered to the ground and two men continued to support him as they stood waiting for the order to move away form the train.

Thanks to the fresh air, every man in Jack's car survived the four-hour trip. Others weren't so fortunate, and Jack watched as dead were dragged to the door openings and unceremoniously pushed out.

When the cars were empty, they ordered the prisoners to form columns and move off up a narrow dirt road. The man with the mangled foot hobbled along with two prisoners on either side supporting him but as they fell farther and farther behind, the guards grew increasingly agitated, menacing the men with their rifles and shouting "hayaku, hayaku." Finally, for their own survival, they lowered him to the ground and walked away. When Jack looked back he saw the man had started to hobble up the dusty road. Jack paused, watching the painful struggle. Before he could go back to help, he was prodded into motion by the point of a bayonet. As he moved off, tears burning his eyes, he struggled to keep from looking back. Too many tragic images had already burned into his mind; he needed no more.

The next two days were the most difficult since they had been captured. Pushed to the very limit of human endurance many were unable to keep up and were either left to die or were executed on the spot. Unlike the flat road between Marivels and San Fernando, which had run along the eastern edge of The Bataan Peninsula, virtually every foot of the road from Capas was uphill.

After a short rest stop on the second day, the march resumed. Jack rose slowly, but Charlie remained seated in the dusty road.

"Come on, Charlie, get up."

"Jack, I can't go no further. Just leave me here and go on."

A wave of anger swept through Jack. With his good arm, he grabbed Charlie and pulled him to his feet.

"Goddamn it, Charlie, you're not quitting now. We've come too far and I'm not leaving you. Get your ass off the ground and let's get moving."

Charlie struggled to his feet and, with his arm around Jack's waist, seemed to gain strength from Jack's resolve.

After another hour's march, the column reached the top of a steep hill and before them lay a large encampment of tin-roofed, wood buildings surrounded by a high barbed wire fence. As they drew closer, Jack could see a sign over the gate-*CAMP O'DONNELL* in large green letters. They had reached their destination.

CHAPTER 14

After they passed through the gate of Camp O'Donnell, Jack saw a long line of prisoners winding its way to a single water spigot. Some men held canteens while others clutched makeshift containers made of old food cans or hollowed-out sections of bamboo. The line snaked around the camp perimeter, disappearing behind a building on the far side.

Jack, turning to Charlie. "Look at that. You could die of thirst before you got to the head of that line." The last word had scarcely escaped Jack's lips when a man-still a long way from the spigot-fell face down in the brown dirt. The men around him knelt, and one taking the man's wrist in his hand, felt for a pulse. Finally, satisfied that the man was dead, two men pulled the fallen man to the side, and without a word got back in line. As the line moved slowly past the dead man, no one even bothered to look down. Jack thought some even looked relieved. After all, those who had been behind the fallen man were now one step closer to the water spigot then they had been before.

Jack couldn't take his eyes from the body. "I think I jinxed the guy."

"Whada mean?"

"I just said you could die before you got to the water and just like that, he ups and dies."

"You saying it didn't have nothing to do with it. He was killed by the goddamn Japs, and nobody else."

Camp O'Donnell was divided down the middle by a broad dirt road. On one side were the barracks for the American and Filipino prisoners; the other side housed the Japanese garrison that manned the camp. After passing through the gate, the new arrivals stood in the hot sun for two hours before a Japanese officer wearing knee high riding boots polished to a high shine emerged from the headquarters building. Pacing slowly, slapping a riding crop against his boot, he began speaking rapidly in Japanese. A subordinate officer stood to one side, acting as an interpreter.

"You are now in the Camp O'Donnell prisoner of war camp. This place was formerly used by the Philippine Constabulary for training their officers who, like you, are now prisoners of the Japanese Imperial Army."

Slapping his riding crop against his leg, "No prisoner of war camp can function without rules and you must obey the rules. Rule 1. There will be no escapes. Violation of this rule will result in execution. Rule 2. You will not steal food. Theft of food will result in withholding your food ration. Rule 3. You will not cross the road separating you from the Imperial Army personnel. Anyone crossing the road will be shot. Rule 4. Each man will be assigned to a work detail and will perform work as directed. No work. No food." Then the officer wheeled and walked back into the building.

The man who had acted as interpreter said, "You will now be assigned to a barracks in which you will live."

A guard started counting off men. When he reached 50, the English-speaking officer said, "Follow that man to your barracks. Remember your building."

As the men were divided up into groups of 50, Jack and Charlie watched anxiously, fearful they would be assigned to different barracks. But once again they were able to avoid separation.

The barracks were run-down wooden structures with rusty tin roofs and peeling paint. The upper half of the walls was open to the elements with only a tattered screen to keep out the ever-present swarms of mosquitoes. There was a screen door at each end and on the floor were thin mats laid edge-to-edge and separated by a central walkway approximately three feet wide. The mats were filthy and blood stained.

When Jack and Charlie had chosen their places, they sank heavily onto their mats.

"Shit," Charlie said, "this thing feels like it's filled with rocks."

Slim had walked behind Jack and Charlie on the road from Capas. "Don't complain. These are the first things we've had between our butts and the hard ground for the last three months."

"He's right. Count your blessings, Charlie," Jack said.

Charlie grunted.. "Oh thank you Mister Jap, sir, for these wonderful accommodations. You're so nice to us poor shithead American GI's."

While the brief moment of levity brought smiles to faces that had had very little to smile about lately, it couldn't erase the reality of their situation.

Even though the sun's heat radiating through the tin roof raised the temperature to inhuman levels, Jack was grateful that the long journey had ended. As he lay back on the hard mat contemplating what a horrific turn his life had taken in the last six months, an American officer entered and asked for the men's attention.

"I'm Colonel Thatcher, the ranking officer here. You've probably already figured out that The Geneva Conventions concerning prisoners of war mean nothing to the Japanese, so the best we can do is stay alive by doing as they say. You have just survived a terrible ordeal on the march from Marivels-and I wish I could tell you that the worst is over-but unfortunately, O'Donnell is a hellhole. We're losing 20 or 30 Americans and three times that many Filipinos every day. Water is scarce. It's not unusual to stand in line for 10 to 12 hours for one cup of water. You'll receive just enough food to keep you alive, but if you can rathole money or cigarettes, there's an active black market. For $5 or ten cigarettes, you can buy a can of fish from the guards. Virtually every man here suffers from some disease. Besides malnutrition and dehydration, many have malaria, beriberi, dysentery, and dengue fever. If you collapse you may be assigned to the hospital. If that happens, don't expect much but there are three good doctors at the hospital who'll do their best for you. The problem is they don't have the medicines and there are too few of them to help all of the bad cases we have here. Are there any questions so far?" No one said anything, so Colonel Thatcher continued.

"Every man able to work will be assigned to a work detail of ten men. Some of the work is hard physically, others are hard mentally. Because of this, I try to give each unit frequent changes in the details. The work you do on these details are for your own benefit and, the better you do it, the better off you'll be. The Japs are masters of psychology. The reason you are part of a ten man group is that they know that each man will work harder and obey the rules if he knows the whole group will be punished if one man doesn't do his part. If one man of a group tries to escape, the whole group will be executed. Because of this, each of you will be asked to sign a no-escape pledge. Same thing if you steal food and get caught. The whole group loses their food ration. Does everyone understand that?"

One man raised his hand. "In training we was taught that it was our duty to try and escape. Now you're saying we can't try even if we want to?"

"What I'm saying is, if you try to escape, your chances of making it are slim at best. You will probably be caught.

If you are, you will be executed and the other nine men of your group will die right along with you. If you're lucky enough to get away, then the nine men you leave behind will be executed. When you were told that it was your duty to try and escape, nobody knew we'd ever be POWs of people with the mentality of the Japanese."

The colonel paused and looked at each of the men before he continued. "I'm going to pass out two papers. One is a no-escape pledge. On the other, put your names in groups of ten. Each group will be assigned to a work detail. If you want to stay with a friend, make sure your names are in the same group."

As the papers circulated, Col. Thatcher looked around to make sure there were no Japanese nearby. Then said in a lowered voice, "I want every man to try and remember the names and faces of the Japs who have murdered, tortured, or mistreated us. We're going to win this war and some of us will get out alive. When that day comes, we'll hang these sonsabitches."

The first assignment for Jack and Charlie was the burial detail, responsible for gathering up and burying the dead. The detail was divided into three groups…one picked up the dead and carried them to one side of the camp. The second group dug the mass graves and the third group did the actual burying.

The first day convinced Jack that picking up the dead was one of the mentally tough jobs the Colonel had talked about. It didn't take much strength to pick up a corpse that was nothing more than skin and bones. But it tore at Jack's heart to see young American GI's-only months ago, nice looking, healthy young men-now lying dead of starvation and neglect, 8,000 miles from home.

Jack got through the first day without going mad by occupying his mind with other thoughts. He thought of Laura and how it would be when they were married and raising a family. He thought about when his high school won the district basketball title and he sank the winning basket as the buzzer sounded. He thought about Mickey, his little terrier. And when he couldn't keep his mind on memories of past, happier days, he said over and over to himself, *"Yea though I walk through the valley of the shadow of Death, I will fear no evil, for thou art with me."*

With practice Jack found he could blank out his present surroundings and become completely oblivious to what was going on around him. He called it his "zombie zone" and he could become so immersed in it that he would be unaware when someone was calling his name. One time a hand forcibly shaking his shoulder brought him abruptly back to the real world.

"Jack, what's wrong with you?" Charlie asked.

"Nothing, why?"

"I must of called you 20 times, and you acted like you never heard me."

"Guess I just wasn't listening."

"You must have been in some deep thought."

"Guess so."

"Well, that's damned sure dangerous. What if a guard gives you an order and you don't do what he says right away? Hell, he'd shoot you before you even knew he was talking to you. I don't know what was so important to think about."

"I was thinking about a little dog I had. His name was Mickey and he liked to ride hanging out the car window. One time when we were going down the highway at a pretty good clip, I looked up just in time to see Mickey's ass disappear out the window. He'd leaned out too far and fell out"

"Did it kill him?"

"When I looked back Mickey had his leg up, pissing on a tree."

Charlie laughed…not a big laugh, but a laugh just the same.

When they found a dead man, the burial detail would try to identify the body, so that maybe someday his family would know what happened to him. Jack had always wondered why there were two identical dog tags on the chain you wore around your neck. Now he knew at least one good reason. Many of the men no longer had their dog tags… they had either been lost or taken by the Japanese…but when they found a body with tags, the burial detail would pry open the mouth and put one tag under the tongue so that the body could be identified if the graves were ever discovered after the war. The other tag was given to Col. Thatcher so the man could be listed on the roll of dead.

On the first day, virtually every man Jack picked up had died of disease. Many had raw, open sores, oozing blood and pus, raising fears of contacting a deadly disease. Careful to avoid the open sores, men of the detail would roll the body in a tattered blanket, tie each end to a pole, and carry it to the burial area.

As the first day ended, Jack and Charlie were appalled at how many dead were lying in a row down the fence line.

A gaunt man with long, matted hair saw Jack staring down the long row and said, "Yours makes an even hundred today."

"A hundred in one day?".

"You must be new here, buddy. We get that many nearly every day. The record since I've been here is a hundred and eight, but I expect we'll break that record pretty soon." Looking down the long row he said. Know what's good about this job?"

Charlie looked to see if the man was kidding. "There ain't nothing that could be good about this job."

"That's where you're wrong, buddy. As long as you're carrying 'em in and burying 'em, then you know you're still alive."

"That's about the dumbest thing I've ever heard," Charlie replied.

"Think about it. Being dead and in Hell couldn't be any worse than this. So how do you know that you're not in Hell already? The way you know, is that by picking up these bodies you know you're still alive here on earth. If you was dead and in Hell, these bodies would be up walking around just like you."

"I never thought about it that way" said Charlie. "You just might have something there."

CHAPTER 15

To keep up with the steady stream of dead bodies, mass graves were dug almost round the clock. The graves were dug 10 feet long and five feet deep. After a body was removed from its blanket, it was placed neatly in the bottom of the pit, with arms crossed across the chest to take up less room. At first, only one layer of bodies was placed in each grave, but as more and more bodies waited for a grave, the burial detail began stacking them, as you would a cord of firewood, until the bodies would be three or four deep. The overpowering stench caused the men to gag, their empty stomachs convulsing with dry heaves.

The daily rains turned the ground into a quagmire. At times, the rain was so heavy that the graves would fill with water causing bodies to float to the top before the hole could be filled with dirt. The burial detail would hold the bodies down with poles while others shoveled dirt on top of them. But, like a scene from a horror movie, bodies would pop back to the surface, as if reluctant to leave their living comrades.

After an interminable week of picking up the dead, Col. Thatcher rotated Jack's group to the water detail. The change came just in time to save Jack's sanity. Some adjusted to the sight of their dead comrades, but Jack never did. Laying on his mat each night staring at the tin roof, the dead marched in an endless procession through his mind. Only when completely exhausted could he fall into a fitful sleep.

There was only one water spigot for the prisoner's and additional water had to be brought from a nearby stream in large metal drums carried by the prisoners. The difficulty in getting the water to camp made it O'Donnell's most precious commodity. It was used mainly for cooking and on the rare occasions when there was any left over, the thirsty men would crowd around the barrel for a sip of the tepid water. There was no water for bathing so the prisoners would stand in the daily rain, faces skyward to wash the grime from their bodies.

The emaciated men he'd carried to their graves sometimes weighed no more than a small boy, but the water drums were very heavy. The water detail were divided into five-man groups...four would carry a barrel, laid across poles...while the fifth acted as a spare to step in for anyone who faltered. They would alternate like this until they staggered into camp with their load. There was one advantage of being on the water detail. While at the river the men could wade into the water to bath and before starting the arduous trek back to camp they would lay on the bank, filling their bellies until they could hold no more.

Life at O'Donnell worsened as more prisoners arrived. Food rations became smaller. Rampant dysentery caused the latrines scattered around the camp to became so foul that the men had to dig trenches that they could straddle to relieve themselves. When the "straddle trenches" filled with watery, often bloody discharge, the prisoners would cover it with dirt and dig another. The men used handfuls of dirt, grass, and sometimes clothing taken from the dead to clean themselves.

Filipinos from a nearby village would sneak up to the fence in the surrounding brush and, when they were sure no guards were near, would toss bread, cooked chicken, potato like vegetables called comoties, fruit, and cigarettes over the wire to the waiting prisoners. Cigarettes were a prized catch, even for those who didn't smoke, because they could be used as barter for food with other prisoners and even some of the guards. One of the more compassionate guards would trade a small tin of fish packed in oil for ten cigarettes. The prisoners nicknamed him "Charlie Chan," because of his resemblance to the popular movie character of that name. When Jack pointed out to one of the other men that the movie actor "Charlie Chan" was Chinese not Japanese, the man said, "Jap, Chink, they all look alike to me."

Jack and Charlie carefully hoarded any cigarettes they were able to get. When they accumulated 20, they would get two cans of fish from "Charlie Chan" and, sitting in their barracks that night would enjoy the smelly fish as if it was the greatest delicacy in the world.

Charlie was still having intermittent attacks of malaria. One time when his chills and fever got particularly bad, Jack went to the hospital to ask for quinine. The prisoners called the hospital *The Zero Ward,* because anyone taken to the hospital never returned. *One man in. Zero out.* Going there was a death sentence…only men who could no longer stand were taken there.

Entering, Jack saw the sick lying silent on their thin, dirty pads. No one was moving. It was as if they were already dead, but there was something else. Jack was used to the smell of decaying dead flesh when bodies in the hot sun began to turn a dark purple, swelling up like balloons. But here in *The Zero Ward* it was different. It was the unmistakable smell of gangrene. The smell of dying men. Most of the men lay on their backs, some with their eyes closed; others stared vacantly at the tin roof. One man feebly waved at the large black flies that buzzed around his head. Jack searched the faces, always looking for a familiar one. As he passed one man who lay partially on his side, he looked back over his shoulder and froze. The face was thinner, the eyes sunken, and there was a nasty wound above the left eye, but there was no doubt…it was Capt. Robert E. Lee Clark. His eyes fluttered open when Jack knelt and said his name. Jack gasped when he saw the black hole where the left eye had been.

"Capt. Clark, it's me, Collins."

Jack had to lean close to hear the barely audible voice. "Collins?"

"Yes sir. Private Jack Collins. A Battery."

"A Battery?"

"Yes sir. A Battery. 201st."

"Oh yes, Collins. A Battery."

With that, a deep sigh escaped Clark's wasted body and he closed his eyes as if to say I'm tired of this conversation.

"Capt. Clark. Capt. Clark." Jack softly touched Clark's arm but got no response. He had so many questions…why had Malloy been tied to the tree and butchered? Were the others dead or alive? But he would get no answers now. Jack knelt beside Capt. Clark for several minutes before he rose and left the building. In another building, a Japanese doctor was examining a Filipino who already looked dead. Jack stood silently until the doctor had finished ministering to the man, then cleared his throat. The doctor turned toward him with a questioning look.

He wasn't sure that the doctor would understand that he needed quinine for a malaria patient. Speaking in *pidgin* English and using hand signals, "*Need medicine.*" Pointing to his mouth. "*Fever.*" Hand on his forehead.

The doctor, whose white coat was stained and soiled with blood, held up his hand. "I received my medical training in California and speak English very well. What do you want?"

"My friend is having severe fever and chills from malaria. Can I get some quinine for him?"

"Quinine is one of the few medicines we have in good supply. Come with me."

The doctor led Jack to the next building where he took a large bottle from a cabinet and handed to Jack.

"Use the cap to measure it with and give your friend a cap full once each day when he is having fever…and try to keep him as dry as possible."

Jack gave the doctor a quizzical look. It was the monsoon season and it impossible for any prisoner to stay dry.

The doctor held out the bottle and when Jack hesitated said, "Go ahead, take it."

As Jack went out the door, he heard the doctor say, "Sorry your friend is sick."

Jack looked back at the doctor and could tell he was sincere, but wondered how he truly felt about Americans. He had lived and studied in America. He probably had friends there. Now here he was, seeing people who had most likely treated him with kindness and respect, suffer and die at the hands of his own people.

When Charlie heard Capt. Clark was still alive and in *The Zero Ward*, he wanted to see him immediately, but became so dizzy when he stood that Jack had to grab him to keep him from pitching forward on his face. Jack gave him a dose of quinine and promised that they'd go see Capt. Clark the next day.

The quinine worked like a miracle and Charlie awoke the next morning feeling refreshed and without the fever or shaking that had racked his body the day before. Charlie was eager to see his commander, but Jack persuaded him to wait until they had received their morning ration of rice so that could share it with Capt. Clark. A little nourishment might just help Capt. Clark do the impossible…leave The Zero Ward alive. Both saved a portion of their rice and hurried to the hospital building.

Jack remembered that Capt. Clark had been near the far end of the building on the right side, but his heart sank when he saw the thin, stained pad empty.

"What happened to the man that was there yesterday?" he asked, kneeling beside the man on the next pad.

The man rolled his head in the direction Jack pointed.

"Was he your friend?"

"He was my commander. Where's he gone?"

"To heaven…maybe hell. He died last night, just like the rest of us are gonna do."

CHAPTER 16

Because they always must be prepared to move on a moment's notice, men at war have few personal belongings. All of Lt. Kenji Tanaka's gear fit easily into a duffel bag, so he was able to pack and hitch a ride on a truck going to Manila on the same morning that Capt. Aoki told him he'd been reassigned. The driver dropped him off in front of Army headquarters located in the former Philippine presidential palace. The palace had been spared damage during the air assaults on Manila. Flags with large red circles on white backgrounds fluttering atop the building were the only noticeable change.

Kenji was greeted in the personnel office by a young officer almost hidden by the papers stacked on his desk.

"I'm Lt. Tanaka, reporting for reassignment."

The young officer scowled at Kenji as if he didn't have time for him.

"Please have a seat," he said.

As Kenji sat in one of the straight back chairs lining the wall, the officer returned to the massive piles of paper in front of him. It appeared to Kenji that he was merely moving papers from one stack to another, and then back again. Finally, after almost an hour-without the officer so much as glancing in his direction-Kenji stood and asked, "Have you found my assignment yet?"

"What was your name?"

"I told you before, my name is Lt. Kenji Tanaka. I was at San Fernando and I was told to report here for a new assignment."

The officer pulled a stack of papers to him and began leafing through them, one at a time, as he said to himself, "Tanaka, Tanaka, Tanaka."

Kenji grew more irritated, wondering how they could be winning the war with such inefficiency.

"Ah yes. Tanaka?"

"That's correct."

"Well, Lt. Tanaka, you are being assigned to the 20th Infantry Division."

"Where are they located?"

"At the former American base, Fort McKinley, right outside Manila."

After leaving the personnel office, Kenji was directed to a motor pool where he was able to find transportation to the former American installation that now housed the 20th

Infantry Division of The Imperial Army. As the vehicle drove onto the base, he noticed a building on which red letters showed faintly through a fresh coat of white paint. It appeared to be an artillery gun pointed skyward, with the numbers 201st in a semicircle below. He turned and stared at the emblem until it had passed from sight, trying to remember where he had seen it before. Then it came to him. It was the same as the patch on the American's sleeve at the warehouse door in San Fernando. What a bizarre coincidence. He was undoubtedly driving down a street on a former American Army post where the tall American soldier with the tattoo on his arm had been stationed. Again he could see the frightened, young face and the tattoo...the beautiful red, white and blue tattoo.

When he entered the building that served as Officer Quarters, he heard someone shout, "Kenji!"

Turning, he saw the smiling face of his friend Kochi.

"Kochi, what are you doing here?"

"Probably the same thing you are. Getting ready to go to war again," Kochi said with a laugh.

"What do you mean, go to war again? I thought we'd been at war since the 8th of December."

"In case you haven't noticed, the war here in the Philippines is over. Now it's on to bigger and better things."

"And where might that be?"

Kochi stepping closer and surreptitiously looking around as if the enemy were lurking around the corner, said in a whisper, "Rumor is we're headed for the Solomon Islands. After that will come Australia, and after that we will rule all of Asia and the entire Pacific"

* * *

The shock of Captain Clark's death had hardly worn off when Jack and Charlie, along with a large group of other prisoners, received word that they were to be moved to a new camp. The news was greeted with mixed emotions. No one was sorry to be leaving Camp O'Donnell. On the other hand, who knew what the next place would be like? As bad as O'Donnell had been, at least it was a known factor and they had learned to cope as well as could be expected.

After being marched back to Capas, the prisoners were loaded in boxcars to be taken to their new POW camp. Jack and Charlie were herded into a boxcar with enough room for the men to sit on the wooden floor. During the six-hour trip, Jack sat with his back against the wall letting the gentle rocking motion and rhythmic clack of the wheels lull him into a deep sleep. When the train slowed to a halt and the door was pushed open, all 60 prisoners in the car had survived the trip. A large white sign on the station told them they were in Cabanatuan.

Marched down a dusty road, the prisoners crested a hill and saw their new home. Located on a flat plain, surrounded by well-kept fields, was a large camp...much larger than O'Donnell. An eight-foot barbed wire fence surrounded the camp and guard towers, spaced evenly around the perimeter, rose 40 feet above the ground. Speculation about the new camp, ranging from the food to the sadistic nature of the guards, swept through the ranks. Considering the treatment they had been subjected to up to now, most feared the worst.

It was soon apparent that conditions at Cabanatuan were slightly better than they had been at O'Donnell. For the first time, the men had enough water to bathe at least once a week. The prisoners were formed into three groups, each responsible for a different aspect of camp routine. Camp Utility did maintenance around the camp, repaired the barracks, and dug drainage ditches and latrines. Camp Supply obtained food from the Japanese and tended fields around the camp where they raised vegetables to supplement their diet. Camp Library provided the men with reading material and published a crude news bulletin filled largely with Japanese propaganda. The Japanese commander believed the propaganda was being disseminated as intended, unaware that it was being worded in subtle ways that told the men it was mostly Japanese lies. Men not assigned to one of the groups were sent outside the camp to gather wood or construct a nearby airfield.

Despite the improvements the men found at Cabanatuan, many things stayed the same. During monsoon season, daily torrential rains turned the ground into a quagmire. The guards were unpredictable, beating the men with shovels, bamboo poles, or rifle butts at the slightest provocation. And food was always a problem. During their first meal after arriving, Jack looked into his bowl and saw a worm in the rice. Dipping his finger into the rice, he picked up the worm and as he started to throw it to the ground, another man, who had been at Cabanatuan longer, shouted, "Don't do that!"

Jack looked up. "It's a damn worm."

"I know what it is, for Christ's sake. If you don't want it, give it to me."

"You gonna eat a worm?" Charlie asked.

"Hell yes. Them worms are about the only protein you'll get around here. You need protein to stay alive."

The next bowl Jack received also had worms. He closed his eyes and gulped down the watery mixture as quickly as he could. The prisoners received two meals a day and they always consisted of the same watery rice with an occasional piece of pork or fish in it and a small portion of vegetables when they were available from the farms. Sometimes there would be a handful of raw spinach, a piece of camote, or an occasional bite of papaya or mango when they could be found in the jungle.

One day as Jack and Charlie sat in the shade of their barracks attempting to get relief from the hot sun, a large dog walked by.

Charlie watched the dog until it was out of sight. "I read one time that they eat dogs in China," he said.

"I've heard that too. Maybe they're good."

"They sure couldn't be any worse than the shit we're getting, "said Charlie. "Dogs are all over the camp at night. I saw three last night when I went out to take a piss."

Jack looked at Charlie. "Whadya getting at?"

"I think we outta catch one and eat it. They come from the village, and the Japs could care less."

That night Charlie squatted in the shadows of the barracks watching for stray dogs. The other men watched through the screen as a small spotted dog emerged from the shadows and stood looking at Charlie as he softly patted his hands together and let out a low whistle. With tail wagging, the unwitting dog trotted close and Charlie quickly scooped it up and ducked through the screen door. One of the men cut the dog's throat with a knife fashioned from a tin can and the hungry men watched as the animal was skinned and cut into small pieces. As soon as it was light enough, the men dug a small pit and using splintered boards from the side of their barracks, built a fire to roast the meat.

"This ain't half bad," Charlie said, wiping juice running down his chin with the back of his hand.

Several others grunted their agreement, but Jack couldn't help thinking about his little dog Mickey. Regardless, it was the first substantial meal any of them had eaten in months.

* * *

They learned that Corregidor had fallen when prisoners from the island stronghold began to arrive at Cabanatuan, first in a trickle and then in a steady stream. Many of the men who had endured the Death March had held out hope that Corregidor could be held until reinforcements could arrive and a counteroffensive launched to rescue them from their Japanese captors. But, they soon learned from the new arrivals that this had never been even a remote possibility. Reinforcements never came, and when they had began to run out of food, ammunition, and medical supplies, General Jonathan Wainwright, who had been left in command when MacArthur was evacuated, had no choice but to surrender. Although the men from Corregidor had subsisted on meager rations and had the same diseases common among them all, they had been spared the march from Marivels, being transported by truck and train to Cabanatuan and had arrived in much better shape than those who had surrendered on Bataan.

With only a few guards to watch the large number of prisoners, escape was a real possibility and, though risky, a constant topic of conversation. At O'Donnell, escape had been discouraged because of the threat to other group members, but here they had not been divided into groups and there had been no threats. So it was no surprise to Jack when he heard that a man named Larry was missing and had probably escaped. For two days, there was no sign of Larry and no sign from the Japanese that they knew he was missing. On the third day, all the prisoners on outside work details were brought back to camp early and assembled with the others in a large open area that was formerly the Filipino Army parade ground.

They were kept standing in the hot sun for over an hour before two guards came from a building leading Larry, a rope tied around his neck, hands bound behind his back. His face was swollen and blood ran from his nose. Unsteady on his feet, Larry fell and the guards continued to drag him through the dust. No one knew where Larry had been for two days or how he had been captured. When they reached a place in front of the assembled prisoners, Larry was hoisted to his knees and a Japanese officer with a long sword stepped behind him and raised the sword high above his head. To Jack, it seemed like an eternity as the officer stood with the sharp blade poised for its deadly stroke. Then, so fast that it was just a blur, the sword swooped down, and Larry's severed head fell to the dusty ground. The men stood silently as Larry's body toppled sideways and, the still beating heart pumped the blood from his body.

Then, the guards dragged another prisoner chosen at random from the assembled men, and the sword-wielding officer swung the glistening blade again. Then another man was dragged from the ranks and then another and another...until ten headless bodies lay before them. The guards stuck the heads on bamboo poles and rammed them into the ground. There they remained until the flesh fell away from the skulls, a grim reminder of what would happen if there were any further attempts to escape.

When the Japanese began to send prisoners into town for supplies, the men picked up bits of information from the civilians. What they heard about the progress of the war was vastly different from what the Japanese had been telling them. The accounts of Japanese victories in China, Malaysia, Burma, and the Pacific islands were soon followed by word that Tokyo had been bombed by a group of B-25's flown from an aircraft carrier. When word of the Tokyo raid reached camp, cheers rippled through the camp. It was a huge boost to moral when they learned that American forces had recovered enough from Pearl Harbor to mount offensive operations.

Then, in June came word of a resounding victory for the United States in a massive naval battle at Midway Island. The Japanese navy had been badly crippled when they lost four aircraft carriers. Japanese propaganda told of a Japanese occupation of the Solomon Islands, but less than a month later, Jack heard while he was in town that the Marines had landed at Guadalcanal and were slowly driving the Japanese back into the sea. It seemed to Jack that each time his spirits were at a low point, good news filtered into camp and his faith would be renewed that one day he would return to marry Laura and settle down to raise a family.

* * *

The Japanese high command considered the Solomon Islands of the utmost strategic importance for control of the South Pacific region. When the 20th Infantry Division landed at Guadalcanal, the first order Kenji's unit received was to set up defensive positions to repel any American attempts to take the islands. A large contingent of construction engineers was brought in to build an airfield from which operations could be conducted throughout the South Pacific and all the way to Australia.

After a long hot day overseeing his men building bunkers overlooking the beaches, Kenji lay on his bunk reading, while Kochi slowly turned the dial on a small radio. Kochi was always excited when he picked up stations as far away as Sydney and Manila. Reception was always much better after the sun went down, and one time he was sure he heard a station give a San Francisco call sign. Now, as he spun the dial through the frequencies, he heard a remarkably clear voice reporting in English on a great naval battle between the American and Japanese navies at Midway Island. Both Kenji and Kochi understood English so it was easy to follow the words. Kenji lowered his book to his chest and turned his head to listen. The voice was talking about a great American victory. The Japanese navy had been dealt a devastating defeat with the loss of four prized aircraft carriers...the *Kagi,* the *Soryu,* the *Hiryu* and the *Akagi.*

When Kenji heard the name *Akagi,* he threw his book aside and moved close to the radio to hear every word. The *Akagi,* was the carrier his oldest friend Takeo had been assigned to. His fears grew as the voice reported that American dive-bombers had scored direct hits on the deck of Japan's premier carrier and it had sunk almost immediately with great loss of life.

Kochi turned to Kenji and said in the bravado tone that Kenji had heard so often, "Don't worry, it's all propaganda. I'm sure your friend is alive and shooting down American planes this very moment."

"Why do you think its propaganda? They even knew the names of our carriers."

Seeing the look of fear on Kenji's face, Kochi said, in a somewhat softer tone, "Kenji, my friend, we have the best equipped and best trained navy in the world. It's all a big lie. The Americans could never deal us a defeat of these proportions…And besides, what could they defeat us with? We destroyed their fleet at Pearl Harbor."

But news about Midway proved true. Days after hearing the radio report, an aircraft landed at the partially completed airfield and a naval officer aboard the airplane told Kenji that the Imperial Navy had indeed lost a large portion of its carrier force. The man, however, could give Kenji no news of Takeo.

Kenji had little time to grieve for Takeo. On 7 August, a little over a month after the 20th Infantry Division had occupied Guadalcanal, American forces landed and the battle for control of the Solomon's began. In the Philippines, the Japanese had always been on the offensive and though the enemy had fought valiantly, Kenji knew they would defeat the Americans. But now the Japanese were on the defensive and the American Marines were a formidable opponent.

CHAPTER 17

The days at Cabanatuan turned into weeks, the weeks into months, the months into years. The guards still committed acts of brutality, there was no medicine, and men still died of disease. There was never enough food, and sanitation was abysmal. Through it all, Jack's goal remained the same…to survive against all odds.

The prisoners developed a remarkable grapevine, getting information about the war from new prisoners, the townspeople of Cabanatuan, and sometimes even talkative guards. The big news came in 1944; halfway around the world, the Allies had invaded Europe and were sweeping across France towards the heart of Nazi Germany. Within weeks of hearing about the invasion of Europe, news came that the Japs had been driven from Guam and somewhere else that Jack had never heard of…a place called Saipan.

In September, the Japanese announced that some of the Cabanatuan prisoners would be shipped to Japan to work in factories and mines. The Japanese freely admitted that this would enable them to put more men in uniform, evidently thinking that this would impress their American prisoners of the growing odds against the United States. But the POW's saw it differently.

Charlie said it best. "They must be in a shitpot full of trouble if they need a bunch of sick, skinny-ass bastards like us to work in their factories."

The Japanese tried to single out the prisoners in the best condition, knowing the sick and weak could perform very little productive labor. Jack was selected almost immediately. Charlie, on the other hand, still suffered from reoccurring bouts of malaria, and was initially passed over, but Jack had hoarded 30 cigarettes for just such an occasion and bribed one of the guards to put Charlie on the list.

Jack tried to be positive about their shipment to Japan. "The way I see it, if you've got a valuable commodity you take good care of it."

"What's that supposed to mean?" Charlie asked.

"Well, they need us to perform labor in Japan. Right? That makes us a valuable commodity. So to get the most work out of us, they'll feed and treat us well."

With a skeptical look on his face. "You think they'll fatten us up, so we can work harder?"

"It makes sense."

"That's where you're wrong, Jack. Nothing makes sense in this place."

The next day, they were marched to the train depot and once again crammed into the old railway cattle cars. Charlie elbowed Jack with his elbow and said, "How do you think they're taking care of their *'valuable commodities'* now?"

The train took them to Manila where they were marched through the streets of the ravaged city to a pier where an old freighter was anchored. After they were herded into three holds, iron grates were pulled over the openings and locked down with heavy chains.

Jack's spirits fell once again when the men were placed in the hot, dark, crowded hold, but once again good news came along to lift it up again. Some in the hold had come from a camp on the island of Mindanao, far to the south of Manila, and told of air attacks by American planes against an airfield there. It was the first time since they had surrendered in 1942 that Jack had heard of American forces attacking the Japanese in the Philippines.

It was late afternoon when Jack felt the ship get underway. As the small patch of light coming through the grate began to fade into darkness, the hold became an agonizing mixture of sound and smell. The roll of the ship on the open sea caused seasickness in many of the men who could be heard groaning and retching throughout the hold. Large metal buckets were lowered for the prisoners to use for their waste, but often they couldn't be reached or passed around fast enough. The smell-urine, feces, vomit, and dirty bodies mingled together- intensified as the suffocating darkness enveloped the men. After the burial detail at O'Donnell, Jack thought he could stand just about any odor, but the air in the dark, dank hold had become so foul that panic began to well up in his chest and he felt as if he would suffocate. Just hours into their voyage the tormented prisoners dubbed it the *Hell Ship*.

The clatter of the chain being pulled from the grate woke Jack from a fitful sleep. When the grate was pulled aside far enough, buckets of rice were lowered by rope to the men below. As he sat eating his meager portion from a tin plate, Jack tried to calculate how long they would have to endure this hellhole before they reached Japan. If it was very long, he feared the weaker men would never survive.

"How far to Japan you think it is, Charlie?"

Charlie cocked his head to one side. "Beats the shit outtaa me. Probably at least a thousand miles."

"Sounds about right," said Jack. "Now figuring this tub can go 15 miles an hour, we should be able to go...lets see, 15 times 24 is ...about 360 miles in 24 hours."

Charlie interrupted. "Boats don't go miles an hour. Boats go knots."

"Don't get technical. We're still going to go 360 miles in 24 hours."

Calculating again, Jack said, "That's three days to go a 1,000 miles."

"Three days in this shit hole. We could die from the stench alone."

A man with heavily tattooed arms and long shaggy red hair said, "There's only one thing wrong with what you say. It's more like two thousand."

Charlie said, "How do you know how far it is?"

"I was a merchant seaman before the war and I was on a freighter that went from Manila to Yokohama. I know it's close to two thousand."

"If you was a sailor," Charlie said, "why'd you end up a damn, dog-faced soldier?"

"I screwed up. Real bad. Waited too long to join the Navy and got my sorry ass drafted."

Jack was disappointed that his three-day estimate wasn't going to hold up.

"How long did it take?"

"As well as I remember, about six days, but that was a helluva lot better ship than this piece of crap we're on now. Wouldn't surprise me none if we don't sink before we get there."

Once again the chain clattered as the grate was pulled back and ten prisoners at a time were allowed to go up to the deck where a guard wielding a hose sprayed each man with a powerful stream of salt water. Though the buckets of waste were carried up and dumped overboard, it did little to improve the foul air the men were breathing.

When Jack finally got his turn to go up the ladder, the fresh air flooded his lungs and once again he felt that he'd been given a reprieve from death. As the powerful stream of water hit him, he had to struggle to maintain his balance, but the cold water was refreshing, washing away the sweat, grime, and smell that permeated every pore of his body. One of the men too weak to withstand the force of the water, fell on the slippery deck. Like a punch drunk fighter, he struggled to his feet only to be knocked flat again. Each time, the guards howled with laughter.

* * *

Kenji's thought the turning point of the war had been the battle of Midway. Not only had he probably lost his good friend Takeo, but within days of receiving that devastating news, the Americans captured the airfield they had worked so hard to build and was using the airfield for operations against the Japanese forces. Although they would win an occasional battle, they were slowly being driven back and he knew they'd be driven completely out of the Solomon"s before long. The jaunty air of superiority that had once been so evident among his men had been replaced by looks of desperation. The tide had definitely turned.

The fierce fighting on land and in the seas around Guadalcanal almost never ceased as the battle for control of the islands wore on. During lulls in the battle, Kenji could hear the big guns of the warships as they dueled in the narrow straits that separated the many islands around Guadalcanal. One day as he led a patrol along the beach, he came upon an area littered with the bodies of Japanese seamen who had been washed ashore after their ship had been sunk. The bodies, as if trying to escape the sea, would surge forward as a wave rolled in and then would lose the ground they had gained when the receding wave pulled them back into the shallow water.

Day after day, Kenji led his men in battle, sometimes surging forward, only to be pushed back by the relentless American Marines. Finally, after more than seven months, the last remnants of the Japanese forces were withdrawn from the Solomon Islands.

Now, on the Island of Saipan, he was once again fighting for his life. He was very tired of this war. Kochi had died on Guadalcanal during a futile battle for a small, insignificant village that no one even knew existed before the war. And now word had come that the American and British armies had landed on the beaches of France and were forcing the Germans back across Europe. Kenji was certain that Japan could not survive if Germany fell.

* * *

The brief respite on deck had rejuvenated Jack, but when he returned below deck, he once again felt himself gasping for air. He knew a lot of it was in his mind, and he took long, deep breaths attempting to quell the panic. He kept telling himself that he wouldn't suffocate, but continued to gasp for air like someone who had just burst to the surface after being underwater too long.

It was worse when it was dark. The entire second night aboard the *Hell Ship* Jack sat on the cold steel floor and forced himself to stay awake, afraid that if he went to sleep he would stop breathing altogether. It bothered him to feel this way, because he had always been able to stay calm under nearly every circumstance. Through the long days of battle and even when the guard had tried to run him through with the bayonet at the warehouse in San Fernando, he had managed to remain relatively calm. Those things happened so quickly there was never time to think. But this was different. Sitting in the dark, suffocating hold gave a man plenty of time to think and the more time he had to think about all of the bad things that had happened and all the bad things that could still happen caused the fear to build like a gathering storm.

As the first rays of dawn came through the grate, Jack was able to relax and breathe easier. As he started to drift off to sleep, a muffled explosion reverberated through the ship. The old ship shuddered, then tilted so sharply that Jack slid across the floor, ending up in a tangle of bodies. The panicked men clawed and hit each other trying to free themselves from the mass of bodies. Jack broke free and, as he tried to drag himself up the sloping floor, a thunderous blast knocked him flat again. As he tried to rise, a great wall of water surged through the hold and he was sucked into a maelstrom of swirling water. At first there had been blinding light and then he was enveloped in complete darkness as the force of the rushing water spun him end over end. At first he fought the force of the water, but then a strange peace came over him as he realized that he was no longer gasping for air.

The brilliant white light caused Jack to blink and shade his eyes. He thought he was dead and the shining light was a beacon lighting his way to heaven. He could remember being thrown about when *the Hell Ship* suddenly lurched like a bucking horse…and then the darkness.

"Hey, Doc, he's awake."

"Go get the Skipper. This is no Jap," said another voice.

A face appeared above him and he felt a cool hand rest lightly on his forehead.

"Welcome to The USS Mackerel."

The face had a short blond beard and blue eyes framed in wire-rimmed glasses. Definitely not Japanese. Turning his head slightly, Jack could see that the man wore the uniform of a United States Navy Officer.

"The USS Mackerel," Jack repeated.

A new face came into view.

"How you doing? I'm Commander Richardson and this ugly guy with the beard is Doc Lewis, our ship's doctor. As soon as you feel like it, we want to find out all about you. No hurry. It'll be awhile before we can get you to a hospital, but I'm really curious on how you got on a Japanese freighter.

"How did I get here?"

"We plucked you out of the water after we torpedoed the ship you were on."

"The Mackerel is a sub?"

"That's right," Doc Lewis said. "But like the Skipper said, we've got a lots of time to talk. Right now you need some rest."

As Richardson started to turn away, Jack grabbed his arm and pulled him close. "Where are the others you picked up?"

Richardson placed his hand on Jack's shoulder. "There were no others...you were the only one"

"But Charlie was right there with me. He would've been right there in the water with me."

"Who's Charlie?"

"My best friend. We went through hell together. The Japs couldn't kill us no matter how hard they tried, and now you're telling me the U.S. Navy killed him?"

Richardson looked into Jack's stricken face. "I'm very sorry. We had no idea American's were on that ship."

"Well, that's just not good enough." Jack tried to rise. "Charlie's out there. You've got to keep looking."

As the doctor and another medic supported Jack in a half sitting position, Commander Richardson said, "Son, there was a lot of fire and we couldn't get to some we saw. You were the only one we could save."

Jack lay back and closed his eyes. They had come through so much together. He'd nursed Charlie through his malaria. They had kept each other going when to stop would have meant certain death. They had shared their food and water when there wasn't enough for even one. And now someone was telling him that Charlie was dead...and he'd been killed by a damn American submarine commander.

* * *

Lt. Commander William D. Richardson, United States Naval Academy, Class of '36, had always been one to follow orders religiously, and his orders for this cruise were to stay in the South China Sea, sinking Japanese ships until he had no torpedoes left. But now his strict adherence to orders was wavering. He still had torpedoes and there were still Japanese ships out there to sink-but for three days now, he had been listening to the story told by Pvt. Jack Collins and, if true, someone higher up needed to know what was going on.

After Collins discovered that his buddy had not survived the torpedo attack, he had laid for four days on a bunk in the sick bay without saying a word. But when he finally started talking, the whole horrendous story flowed out nonstop. The only times he stopped was to eat and sleep.

Richardson encouraged Jack to tell the whole story, knowing the situation of the POW' was of vital importance. But Doc Lewis stepped in and overruled his commander. Collins needed rest. The questions could come later.

Jack stood in the conning tower with Lt. Commander Richardson as the *Mackerel* glided towards its berth at Ford Island in Pearl Harbor. The sneak Japanese attack had occurred three years earlier, but there were still many signs of the damage inflicted that Sunday morning. The most prominent evidence of that day, which President Roosevelt had promised would "live in infamy," was the superstructure of the once proud USS Arizona that still protruded from the water. As they moved past the eerie reminder, Commander Richardson told Jack that 1,177 seaman were still entombed in the watery grave.

Jack was taken to Tripler Army Hospital where he was examined by the doctors and pronounced in remarkably good condition considering what he had been through. He had the ugly scar just above the eagle tattoo on his left shoulder, and his once sculpted physique was a mere shadow of it's self. Then the shrinks and intelligence officers took over. Richardson and Lewis had briefed them but they wanted to hear it directly from Jack. At first there was skepticism that it had happened the way Jack told it... some thought he embellished the more lurid details. But as they watched Jack's face when he described the sight of Sgt. Malloy's body bound to the tree, the scene at San Fernando when Swede attempted to rescue the wounded man from being buried alive, the beheading of the ten men at Cabanatuan, and the note bearing Peggy Scanlon's name and address, they knew it was all true. Skepticism turned to shock, and finally to anger. After four days of seemingly endless debriefings, Jack was finally allowed to rest.

Two weeks later, Jack was flown to Letterman, the large army hospital in San Francisco where his parents, who for three years had believed that he was dead, met him. He was sitting on a sunny veranda when he saw them come up the walk. Standing to greet them, Jack saw the distress on his mother's face when she saw the pajamas hanging loosely from his thin frame.

His father did most of the talking while his mother lightly stroked his hair. His father brought Jack up-to-date on all the happenings since he been gone…but not once did he mention Laura. When Jack finally asked about her, his father was evasive at first, but finally stammered, "Son, Laura got married a couple of years ago."

Seeing Jack's look of bewilderment, he continued, "Everyone thought you were dead, son. Laura had to get on with her life."

His father tried to make light of the situation with little remarks like "Women are just like trains…wait long enough and another one will come along." But nothing he said could overcome the numb, empty feeling Jack felt.

Finally, looking out over the manicured hospital grounds, he said, "I guess you can't blame her. No sense waiting for a dead man."

Since his rescue, Jack had avoided looking in a mirror. He had seen the other men at Cabanatuan and was afraid he looked like them. Finally after a month at Letterman, he mustered the nerve to see how he appeared to others. After six weeks of good food and rest, he had gained 20 pounds and daily sessions on the veranda had added color to his skin, but one thing bothered him when he finally stood in front of a mirror: His eyes. Once, his sparkling hazel eyes with long black lashes had been his most striking feature; they were now dead and lifeless. He didn't look in mirrors much after that. Actually, he had come through it all in pretty good physical shape. Except for the malnutrition, the only sign that he had been in battle was the ragged scar on his left shoulder. But there were the invisible wounds of war. The wounds only men who had been through combat could feel. The wounds that would never heal.

After his parents returned to Texas, Jack fell into deep depression, lying for hours on his bunk, oblivious to those around him. His dreams of coming home to Laura had kept him going during the darkest moments, but now those struggles to survive seemed for naught.

But then another miracle occurred...her name was Mary. A pretty, young Army nurse, with a big smile, beautiful red hair, green eyes, and a tender touch that could soothe the pain and despair felt by all of the sick and wounded at Letterman. Jack and every other GI on the ward fell in love with her the first day she glided through the door. She moved effortlessly about the ward in her starched, white uniform with the funny little cap perched atop her head. Over time, her presence was the most powerful medicine they could receive.

The ward had fifty beds spaced exactly five feet apart and Jack could never escape the sights, smells, and sounds of the 49 sick and dying men surrounding him. The ambulatory patients, like Jack, could go to the canteen, play cards, or watch a movie in the rec room. But sooner or later, you had to go back.

Jack would sit on his bed, watching fascinated as Mary went about her duties dispensing medicine, changing dressings, and finding time to listen if a man needed to talk. One day when she was a few minutes late, he imagined that she had been transferred without telling anyone. That she was off on her honeymoon. That some crazed maniac had abducted her. But then she came through the double doors at the end of the room and all was well again.

After Jack had regained much of his strength, he was given a day pass for an outing in San Francisco. He had never been shy with the girls, but there was a terrible lump in his throat as he approached Mary to ask if she would go to a movie and dinner with him. He was certain that he would stand there like some speechless idiot. To his great relief, he was able to stammer. "I was… uh…I was wondering would you like to go to a movie with me tonight?"

Mary looked up with a bright smile, her green eyes twinkling. "Why yes, I'd enjoy that very much."

The movie was Casablanca and Mary cried and squeezed Jack's hand when Humphrey Bogart watched Ingrid Bergman fly off into the night with Paul Henried. Later they ate seafood at Fisherman's Wharf and, as they talked quietly across the table, both knew they had found someone special. She asked about his life before the war, but carefully avoided any questions about his days as a Japanese POW. That could come later.

In wartime there's always a sense of urgency, not knowing what the future holds. On their third date, Jack proposed. His heart sank when Mary hesitated for what seemed an eternity, but then holding his hand tightly with both of hers she said, "Yes, Jack Collins, I will marry you."

They agreed to marry on the day the war ended. On May 8, 1945, Germany surrendered but the war in the Pacific raged on with American troops pinned down by the Japanese on the bloody beaches of Okinawa. Then came the electrifying news of Hiroshima. The hospital chaplain married Jack and Mary on V-J Day, August 6, 1945, and within a week they were headed for Texas to make their home.

* * *

Kenji had escaped Saipan just hours before the island was overrun by the Americans. When he returned to Japan, he had been given a short leave to visit his parents and as he made his way through Tokyo, he was shocked at the destruction of the beautiful city. The American B-29's had dropped thousands of incendiary bombs every night for weeks with devastating results. The wooden houses had fueled the massive firestorms that swept across the city with such ferocity that heat would cause the metal bridges over the Sumida River to twist and bend into grotesque shapes, sometimes falling with a loud hiss into the water below. People waded into the river hoping the water would protect them from the heat, only to die as it heated almost to the boiling point. His parents had survived the raids thus far, but their home had not. Standing in the street before the blackened ruins, Kenji wondered how anyone could have survived...and his country could ever overcome what this terrible war had wrought.

After his brief visit with his family he had reported for duty at a base near Yokosuka, which guarded the entrance to Tokyo Bay. When Okinawa fell to the Americans on the July 22, 1945 forces all over Japan braced for the invasion which was sure to come. It promised to be a long and bloody battle. But everything changed in early August with the electrifying news about Hiroshima.

PART TWO

JACK'S WAR

1984

They only the victory win

Who have fought the good fight and have vanquished the

demon that tempts within;

Who have held to their faith unseduced by the prize that

the world holds on high;

Who have dared for a cause to suffer, resist, fight—if

need be, to die.

– Io Victis. William Wetmore Story

CHAPTER 18

Jack stood at the window watching rivulets of rain zig-zag down the glass. He glanced at his watch…it was almost 8 a.m., but dark, heavy clouds hanging low over the city made it almost impossible to tell that a new day had begun. This had probably been the longest night of his sixty-two years on earth…sixty-two years that had seen many long nights. His gaze fell on the half empty parking lot five stories below where the night duty nurses, some with rain coats over their white uniforms, skipped around puddles and scurried to their cars after another night of tending to the sick and dying. Early visitors, some with flowers or silver foil balloons hurried to get inside to visit their loved ones. Many would get well, go home and have a long life of good health. Others, he knew, would never leave.

Behind him, Jack could hear the monitor's beeps that told him that Mary was still alive. That was about the only way you could tell…that, and if you watched closely, the slight rise and fall of the sheet covering her frail body. It had been this way for three days now, and he knew that it wouldn't be much longer. She had first felt the lump in her breast almost a year ago and had rushed to see Dr. Berkowitz, their family doctor who had treated every member of the Collins family for the last thirty years. An appointment with a cancer specialist and a painful biopsy confirmed what they already feared. But worse news was still to come…the cancer had already spread to the lungs. Depressed and bewildered, they wondered how this could be, when a mammogram barely six months before had shown nothing. Even the trusted Dr. Berkowitz could offer only the feeblest explanation…"There's a lot that we still don't know about the human body."

A mastectomy had been performed almost immediately, followed by radiation and dreadful chemotherapy treatments that caused her to lose her beautiful red hair and left her so sick after each treatment that she couldn't get out of bed for days.

Jack thought of how ironic it was that they had first met, and would now part in a hospital. She had nursed him back to health and then had been his pillar of support when those dreadful days as a POW came back to haunt him. Mary never showed it at the time, but years later he learned how deeply she had been affected by the sight of missing limbs, burned bodies, and sightless eyes…and how often she had cried herself to sleep after a particularly stressful day on the ward.

Looking around the room, Jack thought about how hospitals had changed since those days at Letterman. Mary's room had soft pastel walls, a framed print of a sunrise over some beautiful, white, sandy beach, and a color TV. At first, she had been in a semiprivate room, but somehow it just didn't seem right for another person...a complete stranger...to see the indignity of losing your life to this evil disease, so Jack had paid extra to move Mary to a private room.

As Jack turned back toward the bed where Mary laid, their youngest daughter Debby quietly entered and walked to the side of the bed. Placing her hand on Mary's cheek, as if she needed to feel some body heat to confirm that her mother was still alive, she turned to Jack.

"Dad, go home and get some rest. You've been here for two days straight."

"I'm OK, I was able to sleep some in the chair," Jack said as he put his arms around Debby and held her tightly.

"Well, at least go get some breakfast," Debby said as she tried to guide him toward the door.

"They'll be bringing your mother's tray soon. I'll eat that."

Jack didn't want to leave because he was afraid Mary might awake and ask for him. He would be devastated to know that he wasn't there when she needed him. She had been there for him at Letterman and he would be here for her now. It was unrealistic to believe that he would ever hear Mary's voice again, but he couldn't help hoping that some miracle would happen and Mary could somehow beat this thing. If Jack's days as a POW had taught him anything, it had taught him never to give up hope.

Debby looked at her father's haggard face and knew that he couldn't take much more of this, but before she could protest further, Dr. Stewart, the oncologist, came in on his morning rounds. Debby always marveled at how matter of fact doctors could be when dealing with death. After a perfunctory greeting, he placed his stethoscope over Mary's chest and listened intently, moving it several times as if he was having trouble finding any sign of life.

Straightening up, he turned to Jack and Debby.

"She's very weak. I believe we should probably go ahead and withhold all nourishment."

"We can keep her on the morphine so that there is no discomfort," he continued.

There it was, Debby thought. The death sentence. No more miracle cures today, thank you. She also had the disturbing thought that her mother could hear what was being said.

"Can we talk about this somewhere else...out in the hall maybe?" she asked Dr. Stewart.

"Of course." Dr. Stewart turned toward the door.

"You sure there's nothing else can be done?" Jack asked after the door closed behind them.

Debby had never really liked Dr. Stewart. He was just too cold and indifferent to suit her, but when she mentioned it to Jack, he unexpectedly came to the doctor's defense. They had been sitting in the fresh air of the hospital courtyard, trying to clear their lungs of the myriad smells found in hospitals. Jack had looked off into the distance, as if seeing some far away time and place.

"You're wrong about Dr. Stewart," he said. "He knows that most of the people he treats will die under his care. If he got emotionally attached to his patients, a little bit of him would die each time one of them died and after a while there wouldn't be anything left. It's tough to lose someone you really care about, but it's tougher when you lose someone and think that maybe you could have done something to prevent it."

Though her father had never talked about his wartime experiences, Debby knew he had suffered horribly as a prisoner of war. Once when she was five or six she had become frightened in the middle of the night and, as she tiptoed down the hall towards her parents' room, she could hear her father weeping softly and her mother's soothing voice. She could only catch snippets of what her mother said…."It wasn't your fault"…"You did everything you could"…"Torture"…"You were so brave." Debby didn't understand the pain her father was in until she was a teenager and her mother told her all of the gory details.

Now when Dr. Stewart looked at Jack, Debby thought she detected a small bit of genuine compassion as he replied, "I know this is very difficult, but there is no hope for Mary's survival. I would not be doing my job properly if I told you otherwise. I do not believe she can survive another 24 hours. When the cancer has spread as extensively as your wife's has, it can go to a vital organ very rapidly."

* * *

Jack never really wanted to think about death that much, so when he got those calls about "pre-arrangement" needs, he always refused to even discuss the purchase of a funeral plan. Now, he regretted not having made some prior arrangements. The process was painful and overwhelming when you were grieving over the death of someone with whom you had shared a major part of your life. Even though he could afford the most elaborate casket, he thought it a monumental waste to spend thousands on something that would be buried in the ground, never to be seen again. But the sales people...they called themselves counselors...made you feel as if you really didn't love the deceased if you tried to purchase a less expensive model. Ultimately, he succumbed to the pressure and bought the $4,000 bronze "Sacred Sanctuary" model, complete with 100% imported silk lining.

With the help of his four daughters, Jack had made it through the whole process and they now sat in the front row of the small chapel at Laurel Wood cemetery. Behind them were various aunts, uncles, and cousins...relatives you only see when someone dies...and the many friends the Collins family had cultivated over the years. Mary's death had been expected, but that didn't lessen the grief.

Many wept quietly, dabbing at their eyes as the minister delivered the service.

Although they attended church regularly, they didn't get closely involved in church activities and the minister really knew very little about Mary but, it was a nice service, with many beautiful flowers and a lady from the church choir sung Mary's favorite hymn.

Amazing grace how sweet the sound
That saved a wretch like me
I once was lost but now I'm found
Was blind and now I see

Somehow, somewhere, Jack was sure that Mary would approve.

A trip to get away from it all came up when they gathered at Cindy's house after the service. Jack could never get over how his four daughters had varied so much in appearance and personality. Rebecca, blond, blue-eyed and resembling his father's sister more than her own parents, was the oldest, an the artist who lived with her artist husband in upstate New York. She did abstract paintings, wrote beautiful poetry, and was so intellectual that Jack often marveled at how his genes could have produced such a wonder. Terry, the second oldest, was the homemaker. She was undoubtedly a Collins, with the characteristic square jaw and dark, wavy hair. She and her husband John lived on five acres outside of Austin, where they had, with their own hands, built a rambling country home. Cindy was the next in line. She also had the Collins look and was the businesswoman of the family. She had married an ambitious young man, and together they had built a profitable auto repair business. And then there was Debby. She was the little mother, a worrier just like his own mother had been, always herding around her two boys, worrying about their grades, girl friends and the other activities that occupied young boys in this day and time. When he looked at pictures of his mother and Debby, when they were both young, the only way he could tell who was who was by the clothes they wore.

Cindy brought up the subject. "Dad, why don't you take a vacation? Go someplace you can relax for a while? Cancun maybe. You could lie around in the sun and rest. Heaven knows you need a rest after what you've been through."

"Yeah," Debby said. "Maybe I'll go with you. I need a rest too. How about Hawaii? I've always wanted to go there."

Rebecca joined in, "Why not come up and stay with Paul and me? With all the trees turning along the Hudson, it's the most beautiful place in the world this time of year."

Jack held up his hands as if warding off an attack. "You know I'm not the type to lie around on beaches, and I'm afraid I'd be bored silly in the hills of upstate New York. The last thing I need right now is to have too much time to think. I have plenty of things to keep me busy. The house needs painting, and I've been wanting to put down some new kitchen tile."

The conversation became more subdued as the reality of what this day meant cast its cloud over them once again. Jack left soon after dinner...he loved his girls, but right now he wanted to be alone. While driving home, he thought again of what the girls had said. Maybe they were right. Maybe he should get away for a while. He hadn't had a vacation since he and Mary had made a month-long trip to Italy two years before. After Mary's' cancer was detected, her seemingly constant radiation and chemo treatments hadn't left much time for any recreation. An occasional movie or a quiet dinner out was about all she could handle. But where to go was the big question. He didn't want to go anywhere that he and Mary had gone together, or any place that might remotely remind him of her.

On the drive home Jack had the radio tuned to his favorite station that played the big band hits from the 40's and 50's and gave the latest news each hour. When the news came on, Jack heard an announcement about a typhoon threatening the Philippines.

It had been a long time since Jack had thought of the place where he had suffered so much. He had tried to keep it out of his mind as much as possible. At first, when he was at Letterman, that was all he could think of day and night. He couldn't keep from thinking about the march to San Fernando, Camp O'Donnell and Cabantuan but gradually, with the help of the doctors, nurses, and most of all, Mary, he had been able to put some of it behind him. His body had healed, but inside the wounds lingered on. The bouts of depression. The devastating lows which would last for days at a time. The terrible nightmares when he would wake up screaming and drenched in sweat had, over time, diminished-but they were always there, just below the surface, ready to rear up and take control of his life. There had been times when he had considered suicide, but knowing how much it would hurt Mary is what always kept him from it. He wasn't afraid of dying, but he couldn't hurt Mary. She had worked too hard to keep him alive for him to take it all away from her in a selfish, cowardly act.

But sometimes, he needed more help than even Mary could give him and he would see a psychiatrist. He had never had much faith in psychiatry, mainly because he always had a hard time thinking in abstract terms...and psychiatry was all about abstracts. With other health issues, you could usually see the problem...the x-ray showing the broken bone, the spot on the lung, or the pus in an infection...but no one could see into the mind to know what a person was thinking. But he also knew that psychiatry had changed a lot since his adolescence, when his grandfather, the kind, gentle man all the kids called Daddy Jim, had gone into a depression after he lost his job during the Depression. Now his condition would be treatable with medications not available then, and he could have been completely cured. Then, however, people said he had gone "crazy" and one-day two big deputy sheriffs in dark suits and black hats had appeared at the door to cart him off to the "insane asylum." Jack was never sure what they did to him there but when he came home, the once proud, self-educated man just shuffled around the house in his underwear, wringing his hands, and muttering about how he had been let go from his job as an engineer after so many faithful years.

He had heard somewhere, probably from some shrink at Letterman, that the best way to beat your demons was to meet them head on. Maybe the way to free himself from his demons was to go back to the Philippines and see for himself how things had changed. No more death and destruction. No more pain and suffering. No more brutal Japanese guards. No more lines of emaciated American soldiers stumbling down the dusty road under the searing sun. He could fly to Manila, rent a car, drive around Manila Bay and then down the Bataan Peninsula to Mariveles, where he had started his walk to hell. The walk that became known as the *Death March*.

CHAPTER 19

"Welcome aboard."

The smiling young flight attendant greeted Jack as he strode through the door of the big *PAN AM* jet. This was the third leg of his journey. The first two...Dallas to Los Angeles and then on to Hawaii...had been uneventful under cloudless, azure skies. The stop in Hawaii had been barely long enough to get off and stretch his legs for a few minutes before the long flight to the Philippines. Jack remembered the last time he had arrived in Hawaii standing in the conning tower of *The Mackrel*. It had been many years before but in ways it seemed just like yesterday.

"Thank you," Jack said as he searched for seat 17D.

He had crossed the Pacific twice before. The first time, a ship was taking him, a young, healthy man, to war. The second time, he was on a U.S. Navy hospital ship in such deplorable condition that he wasn't sure he would survive the trip. But he had survived...and now 42 years after those horrific years of World War II he was going back to where it had all happened. The years had been good to Jack. The relatively few wrinkles in his face belied his age, and at 62, he weighed only a few pounds more than when he enlisted in the army. His dark hair was graying around the temples, but Mary always said it made him look more distinguished. He jogged 3 miles every morning before breakfast, could do 100 sit-ups, and bench press more weight than most men half his age.

Jack was pushed back in his seat as the Boeing 707 accelerated down the runway. Circling to the west, Jack looked out of the small window, and saw a ship, sailing west, trailing two feathery lines of white on the dark water. A low hiss sounded in his ears as the jet knifed through the sky and air from the vent above his head was cool and refreshing. Pulling down the plastic curtain that covered the window, he lay his head back against the starched white cloth on the head rest and thought of the last time he had headed for the Philippines.

The voice on the intercom jolted Jack awake. "Ladies and gentlemen, the pilot has started our descent to Manila Airport. Please stow your snack trays, raise your seats to their upright position and make sure your seat belts are fastened securely."

Leaning forward, Jack pressed the button on the armrest. Looking out all he could see was greenish gray water covered with whitecaps but as the plane continued its descent mountains rose through the haze. Then a small island came into view.

"That's Corregidor." The words were eerily familiar. The same words he had heard from the mouth of Master Sgt. Malloy as they sailed into Manila Bay in 1941. The speaker this time was the paunchy man seated next to him. "Went out there on a tour the last time I was here. That's where our guys holed up during WW two."

"Were you in the war?" Jack asked.

"Me? Hell, no. I was too smart for that. Got myself classified 4-F."

"Really?"

"They didn't need me anyway. Them damn Japs bit off more they could chew when they attacked us. We whupped their asses good from the git go. How bout you? Was you in the army?"

"For awhile."

"Well, it looks like it didn't do you no harm."

Jack stared at the man's florid face for a moment, then turned to look out the window again. As he watched

Corregidor disappear under the wing, he wondered again if he should be returning to this place.

* * *

Tanaka-San swiveled his chair so that he could see out over his beloved city. The office of Chief of Detectives for the Tokyo Metropolitan Prefecture was on the fifteenth floor of the Government Office Building in the Shinjuku District. It was one of the most imposing buildings in the city and of the many perks that came with being a fairly high ranking government official, Tanaka- San thought that this large office, with its mahogany desk, original art adorning the walls and his view from the window, were probably his most cherished.

Yes, he thought, he had risen about as high in his life as he was going to go and now it was time to sit back and take it easy. With only a month to retirement, he was looking forward to spending more time with his family and traveling to areas of Japan he had never seen. Or maybe even doing a little foreign travel. Except for his assignments during the war, he had never been outside of Japan. He had read about other countries and was fascinated by the world's diversity. He wanted to see the Grand Canyon, the great pyramids of Egypt, the Amazon. But first, Japan. His country had some of the most beautiful scenery in the world and now he would have more time to travel around the country pursuing his hobby of painting those beautiful landscapes. Over the years he had gotten quite good and knew that if he really had time to work at it he could sell enough of his paintings to supplement his retirement income and live a comfortable life. What more could a person ask than to make money doing something he really enjoyed?

When he came out of the army at the end of that disastrous war, he had little purpose in life. His country had been led into the war by a group of militaristic leaders who were convinced that Japan's destiny lay in expanding its sphere of influence throughout Southeast Asia. Because of them, his people had suffered greatly and would probably never recover from the scars left by the war, and most assuredly, they could never recover from the horrors of Hiroshima and Nagasaki.

At first, he had been enthusiastic about being in the army with its proud tradition of the *Samurai* but it wasn't long before he began to question the concept of loyalty unto death that was instilled in each man. It seemed such a great waste of fine young men to see them charge into the face of certain death.

On his return to Tokyo he was shocked at the devastation. Buildings were blackened heaps of rubble. Some would have one wall standing, or empty holes where windows and doors had been. The Imperial Palace was the city's only undamaged building, purposely spared by the American bombers

He had always believed the Japanese to be a kind, compassionate people, but some of the things he had seen done to captured enemy soldiers had made him ashamed to have been a member of the Imperial Army. He had never abused anyone and had done his best to prevent such things from happening. But he knew that just by being there he was as guilty as those that committed the atrocities. He would bear this personal scar for the rest of his life.

After the war, he had little thought of becoming a policeman. Before the war, the police were just another arm of the military. But after encountering an old friend from school days, who had joined the Tokyo Metropolitan Police Department, he learned that it was different now. His first assignment was to a *koban,* one of many police boxes scattered all over Tokyo. It wasn't until he had single-handedly apprehended an armed robber that he came to the attention of his superiors. After that, his progress through the ranks had been steady but not spectacular, and he had been Chief of Detectives for the last five years. Gazing out over the city, he could see the Imperial Palace surrounded by its moat and park-like grounds and in the distance the Tokyo Tower. Could he ever adjust to life without a view?

* * *

When Jack had first thought about returning to The Philippines, he had been apprehensive but he told himself over and over again there was nothing to fear. After all, more than 40 years had passed since the dreadful *Death March*, his days as a POW, and the sinking of *The Hell Ship*. He'd finally convinced himself that it was just another trip, but as soon as he'd left Hawaii, his apprehension returned. When he closed his eyes, he saw the faces of Charlie, Dick, Bobby, Buster and Enos. He saw Malloy tied to the tree and Capt. Clark lying on the filthy pad at O'Donnell. He wondered whether Sgt. LeBeau had ever reached freedom. Then he saw the Japanese guards...the sword-wielding officer who had beheaded the men at Cabanatuan, the one they called the Toad, but especially the one at the warehouse door thrusting his bayonet at his chest. But as long as he lived, he would never forget the face of the tall Japanese officer who had deflected that deadly blade. As he lay on the ground looking up, he saw something in the man's eyes that set him apart from the others. He had seen the same look in Mary's eyes the first time she had seen his emaciated body at Letterman...compassion for a fellow human being.

* * *

Chief of Detectives Kenji Tanaka shuffled through the papers on his desk but had difficulty concentrating. Only one month until a distinguished career with The Tokyo Metropolitan Police Department would come to an end. He had seen many changes in those years. When he had first become a policeman, the crime rate in Tokyo, had been very low. People never locked their houses or cars. The few murders were usually committed in a moment of passion. Drug and alcohol abuse were rare, and most policemen didn't carry guns. Now it was different. The papers he had on his desk attested to that. One was a report on a murder committed during an armed robbery of a small sushi restaurant. Another was about a drug ring suspected of countless killings across Japan. And in the top drawer of his desk was a Smith & Wesson .38 caliber semi-automatic that he carried in a shoulder holster when he ventured from his office on police business. During the war he had seen enough guns to last him a lifetime. Although he had fought in many battles during the war, he was not certain that he had ever killed anyone. When an enemy fell, you could never be sure whose bullet was responsible. He could say with certainty, however, that he had prevented someone from being killed. And of that he was proud.

Often over the years, the scene at the warehouse door in San Fernando returned to him again and again. He would see the guard knocking the American to the ground and thrusting his bayonet towards the man's chest. Then he would reach out and deflect the blade so that the American received only a wound in his shoulder. As the man's friend ripped away the sleeve that had a patch showing an artillery gun with red numbers, he saw the tattoo of the red, white, and blue eagle.

* * *

After claiming his baggage, Jack hailed a taxi outside the main terminal. As he got in he told the driver, "Hotel Pacific."

He had chosen that hotel because its brochure said it overlooked Manila Bay and and on a clear day you could see the Bataan peninsula.

The driver, a small, olive-skinned man wearing a bright flowered shirt and a New York Yankees baseball cap looked back at Jack with a wide smile. "Yes sir, boss, Hotel Pacific," then he raced away from the curb, weaving in and out of the heavy airport traffic, constantly blowing his horn at anyone or anything that got in their way.

"Can we drive by the waterfront on the way to the hotel?" You know, where the ships dock."

"You want to go by the waterfront? "Sure, boss. We can do that. But it cost you extra."

"No problem." Jack paused as he looked at the driver's identification card on the visor. "Ramon. I want to go by where the ships dock."

"You got it boss."

He wanted to see if he could find the place where he had disembarked when he had first arrived in the Philippines, but even more he wanted to find the place he boarded the *Hell Ship.* That would be his first step in cleansing his mind of the demons left from those awful days. It was funny that he never even knew the name of the ship that had almost cost him his life, and probably was the watery grave of his best friend.

When he saw a sign that said "Pier 21," he asked Ramon to pull over. Getting out, he walked to the edge and looked down at the almost black water. This could be the spot, he thought. He didn't really know but it didn't matter. It was close enough. As he stood looking over the bay, he could see Bataan in the distance, rising above the water.

Jack stood motionless gazing across the bay until the rumble from a passing truck broke his reverie.

Turning, he walked back to the taxi and getting in said, "Let's go to the hotel."

When Ramon pulled up to the hotel Jack asked Ramon if he could pick him up the following morning and drive him around Manila.

Ramon smiled broadly, "You got it, boss."

In his reservation request to the Hotel Pacific, Jack had asked for a room on the top floor overlooking the bay. As the bellboy drew back the curtains, he could once again see Bataan across Manila Bay. Standing transfixed he stared at the land that had transformed him from an innocent young boy to a man aged way beyond his years.

The next morning, Jack walked out of the hotel promptly at nine. True to his word, Ramon was there, leaning against his cab with the ever-present smile on his face.

"Hey, boss. I told you I'd be here and, when Ramon gives his word, you can bet on it. Where we go today?"

"Let's just drive around. I want to see what Manila looks like now."

As they pulled away from the curb Ramon leaned to his right so that he could see Jack in the rear-view mirror. "You been Manila before?"

Jack was silent for a moment then said, "A long time ago."

As they moved through the streets, Jack searched for anything recognizable but there were no bombed-out buildings, no burnt trucks, no anti-aircraft guns pointing skyward. No signs that the city had ever been ravaged by war. It wasn't until they reached the part of the city where bars lined the streets and girls stood on corners that he thought he had been here before. It looked just the same now as it did when he, Enos Charlie, Buster, Dick, and Bobby, the whole bunch, had staggered into the tattoo parlor that Saturday night so long ago. The signs were different and the buildings were new, but he knew this place.

From the moment he had decided on this trip, Jack had planned to visit all of the places where he and his buddies had lived, fought, and died during those terrible years. After returning to the hotel he spread a map out on the bed and those places came vividly to life. Baliuag, where he and Lucas had watched the tanks fight to control the small village. Route 5 crossing the Pampanga River at Calumpit. Bold, black letters marked San Fernando as a major city now, and the railroad to Capas was clearly marked. Running down the coast of Bataan was Route 7 to Mariveles, where the nightmare had started. Clark Field…now Clark Air Force Base…was marked on the map with the outline of an airplane. He knew Camp O'Donnell was north of Clark, but wasn't surprised when he couldn't find it on the map. It was a place best forgotten by everyone. Tracing the path of the Pampanga with his finger, Jack found Cabanatuan. Carefully he highlighted each place with a red marker. Then he drew a line from Mariveles, through San Fernando to the spot where he believed O'Donnell had been, then up the railroad to Capas and Cabanatuan. That had been his journey then and that would be his journey now…a journey he felt he must make to rid his mind of the horrible memories that still haunted him.

The rental car arrived at the hotel at 9 AM as Jack had requested. The first place he wanted to go was Fort William McKinley.

When he had asked Ramon about it. "Hey Boss. There's no place with that name. I drive taxi all over. No place named that."

When neither the man at the front desk nor any of the bellhops knew of Fort William McKinley, Jack wondered if he was confused about the name. Then it occurred to him that none of the people he had asked were old enough to even have been born when the war started. Finally, an older man at the lobby newsstand remembered the name.

"Oh yes, it's a cemetery now. Many men from the war are buried there."

The old man's hand-drawn map was difficult to follow but after a number of wrong turns Jack finally came to a gate that said *Fort Bonifacio World War II Manila American Cemetery and Memorial.* The name was different, the drab, cream-colored buildings were gone, and concrete had replaced the dusty roads, but Jack knew instinctively that this was the place. Driving through the gate, Jack could see row upon row of white crosses surrounding a beautiful white building and an American flag fluttering in the gentle breeze,. Tropical flowers and shrubs, surrounded the field of simple white crosses. Jack thought it was probably the most beautiful place a person could ever hope to spend his life after death.

When he was a boy his family attended church regularly and he rarely missed Sunday school but he never gave a lot of thought to religion. Going to church was just something all good families did. He knew some people just attended church for show. He remembered a wealthy lady who always sat in a pew near the front and would wait until the last minute to make her entrance so that everyone could see her fur coat and jewelry. But his attitudes had changed. Since his experiences in the war, he firmly believed that there was a higher power and he *knew* he had seen his guardian angel in the form of the Japanese officer at the warehouse door in San Fernando.

Parking the car, Jack moved down row after row of crosses reading the names, many simply marked "UNKNOWN." At these, he would pause and wonder about the person buried there. The person wasn't really unknown…he or she was known to someone. A mother, father, friend or maybe a wife knew who this person was. And he wondered, as he had so many times over the years, about the fate of his friends. Was this the grave of one of them? Were any of them alive? After his release from Letterman, he had tried, with little success, to learn their fates. He had been successful in locating Dick's and Bobby's families, but they only knew that the army had classified the men as missing in action. Then they asked the question, "How did you make it and they didn't?" Just like that, guilt was heaped on the other emotions he carried from the war. Maybe it was unreasonable to feel guilt for having survived while his friends died but, that was the way he felt.

Throughout the years, Jack had clung to the belief that someone beside himself *must have* survived. How could he have been the only one? There was Capt. Clark and Malloy, of course...he had seen them. If some of the others had been captured, why hadn't they been liberated when the war ended? There had been persistent rumors over the years that the Japanese had not freed all POWs, that some were still being used as slave labor. In a recurring nightmare he could see Dick, Bobby, and Enos, ankles manacled, laboring in a dark mine shaft. They had been kept in the dark hole so long that their skin had become translucent, completely colorless. Their hair and eyes had lost their pigment making them look like the albino rat he had as a boy. He would awake, soaked in perspiration, when they would turn in unison and look at him with their colorless eyes. He had located Peggy Scanlon in the Chicago phone book and when he called and told her of her husband's fate, he could hear the relief in her voice as she finally found closure.

Jack lingered in the cemetery until early afternoon. Seeing all of those white crosses was an emotional experience and he would stop in front of a cross, staring as if he thought hard enough he could visualize the person that lay there. A plaque in the building said 17,206 men and women were buried there, all killed in the Philippines and New Guinea-but he knew few if any had been POWs. The fate of POWs killed by the Japanese was to be piled in mass graves without anything...a prayer, or simple marker to show they'd ever existed.

Winding his way back through Manila, Jack finally found the highway that ran north up the east shore of Manila Bay. The last time he had traveled Route 3 was during the futile attempt to stop the Japanese advance on Manila. The highway had changed little in the intervening years: it was still two lanes and crowded with vehicles.

In 1941, the traffic clogging the narrow road had been cars, trucks, buses, ox carts and, even people pushing wheelbarrows piled high with all of their worldly possessions. Now, it was cars, trucks, and buses but the going was almost as slow as it had been then. At Plaridel he picked up Route 5 to Baliuag. He wanted to go there first and then work his way back over the path of their retreat to Mariveles.

The thing he remembered most about Plaridel was the little schoolhouse where General Wainwright had maintained his headquarters during the retreat. He could see it in his mind just like he saw it that night the convoy of trucks had stopped and Col. Moore had gotten out of his jeep gone inside. Now, as he drove through Plaridel he didn't recognize a thing. He hadn't expected the schoolhouse to still be there, but he'd hoped that its historical importance would have saved it. Even though Baliuag was only a short distance up Route 5 from Plaridel and he could have easily driven on, it was late afternoon so he decided spend the night at the small Hotel Plaridel.

A tour bus with the words *Nippon Overseas Tours* on it's side was parked in front of the hotel, and when he entered the lobby he saw a large group of Japanese tourists crowded around a young Japanese woman. Holding a sheet of paper above her head with one hand and pointing to it with the other, she spoke rapidly in a high, shrill voice. Most of the Japanese tourists had a camera dangling from a strap around their necks, and those in the rear stood up on their toes to better see and hear the young guide. Jack thought of leaving because he had never completely gotten over the feelings he had toward the Japanese for their inhuman treatment of American prisoners. He had met and dealt with Japanese since the war, but they had usually been born in the United States, and he considered them more as Americans with a Japanese ancestry. But this was different. These people in the Plaridel lobby represented a country that had committed horrible crimes against him and his comrades, crimes that he could never forget. He tried to convince himself that no one in this group had even been born until well after the war and had nothing to do with the atrocities. It would be stupid to let them run him off. No. Japanese or not he would stay.

While working his way around the group in an attempt to reach the front desk, he saw a Japanese man standing apart from the main group. He was short, powerfully built, and dressed completely in black. The first thought Jack had when he saw the man was his striking similarity to the brutal *Death March* guard they'd called The Toad. If you changed the black suit for a khaki uniform, he could be the man's double. Admittedly, he was too young to be the savage guard but Jack had the wild thought that he must be the man's younger brother, or maybe his son. The man turned slowly toward Jack with such a malevolent look that he was instantly swept back in time, and instead of a man in a black suit he clearly saw the brutal guard menacing him once again. Unnerved, he thought again of leaving, but finally with great effort he convinced himself that he wouldn't let them beat him again.

After registering Jack went directly to his room, emotionally drained. In the darkened room he fell across the bed fully clothed and lay listening to the soft whir of the ceiling fan above his bed. Once again the awful images returned and he began to doubt the wisdom of this trip. The whole idea in returning here was to rid himself of the bad memories, but it seemed that bad memories were all he had. Finally falling into a fitful sleep, he awoke only when the sun was well above the horizon. Dressing hurriedly, he rushed downstairs and was relieved to see a nearly empty lobby and the bus no longer in front of the hotel.

Jack reached Baliuag before noon and drove slowly through the small town. The nipa huts had been replaced with more modern buildings, but little else had changed. He drove straight through town to the bridge that crossed the Angat River. Parking at the far end of the bridge where the road disappeared into the trees, he looked back and saw the high ground where he and Lucas had lain directing the artillery fire at the approaching Japanese. His skin crawled when he realized he was standing in almost the exact spot where he had first seen a Japanese soldier. Until then the war had been fought at a distance: it was here, for the first time, that he had seen the face of the enemy.

As he stood staring at the bridge, he felt that someone was watching him. Turning, he was sure he saw the figure of a small man with oriental features duck behind a tree. He stood staring into the dense foliage but saw nothing. Was he imagining things or was someone really there? A hunter? A woodcutter? But then he recalled the story of a Japanese soldier who had been found on Guam more than 20 years after the war. He had refused to surrender and had been hiding in the jungle for all those years. Was there a Japanese soldier hiding in the jungle around Baliuag still fighting his own war? Jack wasn't sure if he had really seen someone or whether his mind was playing tricks on him, but he did know that he suddenly wanted to leave this place.

Hunched over the steering wheel, Jack raced back down the road through Palidrel, and intercepted Route 3 once again, crossing the bridge over the Pampanga at Calumpit. Safely across he stopped to look back up the road, to see that no one was following him. Then, looking down at the river, his mind flashed back to that day when he had watched the Japanese soldiers, under withering fire from the Americans, charge down the bank and force their way across the river. Today the water was steel gray...that day it ran red with blood.

Arriving in San Fernando, Jack stopped at the first hotel he saw, and after checking in went straight to his room. He wanted to find the depot where they had been loaded into the boxcars and he wanted to see if the warehouse was still there. But not now. He would go to Marivels first so it would all be in the same sequence as it was in 1942. The depot was probably the single most important place on his journey-the place where the tall Japanese officer had saved his life. That moment, he believed, had preordained that he would survive the war.

Weary after another restless night, Jack zeroed the trip meter on the car's odometer as he pulled away from the hotel in San Fernando. He had never known how far they had marched from Mariveles to San Fernando.

As he neared Marivels, he saw an airport to the west of the road and knew it was the place where the Japanese had gathered all of the prisoners before the march. He had traveled 55 miles from San Fernando. In 1942 it had seemed like a 1000. 55 miles of asphalt splashed with blood.

Parking beside the road, Jack laid his head back on the headrest and tried to steel himself for the return trip to San Fernando. He was about to start the most difficult part of his journey. Every mile would be filled with horrible memories, but he believed that by reliving those 13 days he could finally close that chapter of his life.

He awoke to the sound of tapping on his window. The air in the car had become stifling, and his shirt was soaked with perspiration. As he raised his head, he was startled at the sight of a uniformed man peering through the window. He lowered the window and the man said, "You all right, sir?"

Now Jack could see the police badge pinned to the man's breast. "Yes. Yes. I'm fine. I just stopped to rest... must have fallen asleep."

"I thought you might be ill."

The man touched the bill of his hat and turned away as Jack started the engine. Glancing at his watch he saw that he had slept for more than an hour. Easing the car into drive he started slowly up the road.

It was impossible for Jack to recognize exactly where he had seen the first man fall, but he thought it had been only a few miles into the march. After driving three miles, he stopped and got out to study the asphalt surface, as if he could find the spot where the man had died. There was a dark stain on the road and he wondered if, after thousands of rains, blood could still be visible.

As he drove on he tried to pick out where he and Charlie had joined up with Sergeant LeBeau and Lt. Carson during the retreat. Where Mallloy had been tied to the tree. Where Colonel Scanlon had waved as they walked away. The places they stopped for the night.

A faded sign along the side of the road told Jack that the first village he came to was Cabcaben and he was sure it was the place they had stopped at the end of the first day's march. Then it had been little more than a few houses clustered along the road, now there were stores, service stations, several restaurants, and a small hotel. Then he saw it again... the same bus he had seen in Plaridel. It was parked in front of a restaurant that served authentic Japanese food. *Nippon Overseas Tours.* was written in large red letters on the side.

Jack made a U-turn, and driving back, parked directly behind the bus. Getting out of the car, he went to the front of the bus and, seeing no one on board, turned and looked at the entrance to the Japanese restaurant. Gold Japanese symbols adorned the black painted windows and although he knew the interior was filled with the Japanese tourists he had seen at the hotel, he felt compelled to go inside.

Dozens of shoes were lined up in the entryway and paper lanterns hung from the ceiling of the dimly lit interior. The Japanese were seated on Tatami mats at low tables, eating with chopsticks from small flowered bowls. The air was filled with high, excited voices, but when Jack entered every face turned toward him and a hush fell over the room. Jack knew immediately that he had made a mistake in entering the restaurant and thought of leaving. Before he could turn to leave, however, a small Japanese man with a white shirt and black bow tie approached, bowed deeply, and motioned for Jack to follow him to an empty table at the rear of the long, narrow room. The man pulled a chair away from the table, handed Jack a menu and bowed again as Jack was seated. With furtive glances in his direction, the talk gradually resumed, but Jack noticed a difference... a subdued mummer had replaced the spirited chatter that filled the room when he entered.

Looking around the room, Jack saw the man whose appearance had brought back terrible memories of The Toad. He was seated at a table in a dimly lit corner of the room with a man whose gray hair overlapped the collar of his shirt. Even though he sat slouched over, Jack could tell he was larger than the average Japanese. As he watched the two men, a waiter went through the swinging door and, while it was partially open, Jack caught a brief glimpse of a man bent over a sink washing dishes. There was no doubt he was Caucasian. Like the man who sat with The Toad his shaggy hair was gray.

Another waiter opened the door and then turned to speak to someone in the kitchen. As he stood with the door partially open, Jack had a long look at the man with the gray hair. As he watched, the man looked up and their eyes met. In that fleeting moment Jack was sure he detected a look of desperation, a wordless plea for help. When a Japanese cook saw Jack staring at the man, he quickly pushed the waiter aside and closed the door.

Why, Jack asked himself, would a man like that be washing dishes in a Japanese restaurant in the Philippines? Rumors had persisted for years that some POW's were never repatriated and were still being held as slave labor. Were the rumors true?

Jack sat in stunned silence, convinced that the man was being held against his will. All eyes once again turned in his direction as Jack rose and his chair scraped noisily on the wood floor. Hurrying to the door, Jack tried to push it open, but the man who had shown him to his table blocked his path.

"Sorry. Can no go in kitchen."

Trying to edge around the waiter, Jack said, "I want to see the American you're holding in there."

"No American in kitchen."

Jack's voice rose, "I saw him through the door. Let me by."

When the Japanese man failed to step aside, Jack pushed him aside and rushed through the swinging door.

The people in the kitchen looked up with startled expressions. One brandished a long knife toward the wild-eyed American. Jack stopped abruptly and looked in desperation for the American but the only people in the kitchen were the Japanese cooks. Bewildered, Jack turned and ran from the restaurant. As he leaned against the door, breathing heavily he could hear the excited chatter of the people in the restaurant return.

* * *

Inside the restaurant, the man who resembled The Toad walked to the man who had blocked Jack's path to the kitchen, and speaking in Japanese said, "The American is either drunk or crazy. Did he saying something about an American in the kitchen?"

"He said we were holding an American in the kitchen."

The short, powerful man in the black suit, whose name was Kenda and in fact was a supervisor with The Nippon Overseas Tour Company, looked past the restaurant owner to see only the five Japanese cooks in the kitchen.

"That American. I've seen him before. He was at the hotel in Plaridel."

"How did he seem then?"

"He acted odd then also."

* * *

Jack started the engine, and drove away, but he had no intention of leaving. Circling the block, he pulled into an alley where he had a view of both the restaurant and the bus. Minutes later the tourists filed out the door and began boarding the bus. After they were all aboard, the gray-haired man he'd seen across the room emerged followed closely by The Toad. Jack was certain he was an American. Walking, zombie like, head down with a slow, shuffling gait, he grasped the chrome bar, struggled on board and settled into the driver's seat. The Toad sat directly behind him. Was the bus driver another captured American being held for slave labor? Why else would an American be driving a group of Japanese tourists? Why would a man, who looked and acted like a guard, be watching his every move? If there were any doubts remaining in Jack's mind about the astounding truth he had come upon they were now completely erased.

Jack knew he could do nothing about the man in the kitchen. Somehow they had outwitted him but maybe he could help the bus driver. When the bus pulled away, he followed it north on the road to San Fernando. It would do no good to go the embassy in Manila. They probably wouldn't believe him. The government might already know and had chosen to ignore it all of these years because Japan was such an important trade partner. Something like that wouldn't be unheard of in the world of international politics. He thought of going to the military at Clark Air Force Base, but what could they do? Start another war with Japan? The local police? They'd just think he was another crazy American. No, it was up to him. If the American slaves were to be rescued he'd have to do it himself.

Traffic was heavy as the bus neared San Fernando. Several times other drivers cut in between them, and fearing he would lose sight completely he decided the only chance he had of rescuing the driver was to force the bus off the road and demand that the American be released.

Drivers glared and honked as he cut in and out of traffic attempting to overtake the bus. As he drew alongside, furiously blowing his horn and gesturing for the bus to pull over he could see The Toad, a scowl on his face, looking down at him and finally reaching up and tapping the driver on the shoulder. As the bus came to a stop, Jack ran to the front, where The Toad blocked the door.

"Let me on. I want to talk to the driver."

"This is a private bus. Leave at once."

Jack tried to see around the wide body but could only see the driver's legs and his hands on the wheel. When Jack tried to board the bus The Toad pushed Jack to the ground.

"If you don't leave at once, I will call the police."

Unable to force his way past the powerful man, Jack ran out in front of the bus where he could maybe communicate with the driver. When he looked up through the wide windshield, he was puzzled to see a young Japanese man sitting in the drivers' seat. They had done it again-just like at the restaurant-they had somehow made the American prisoner disappear. As he stood staring up, the door closed and the bus started rolling forward. Jack, hands pressed against the windshield as if he could halt its movement, walked backwards as the bus inched forward, finally jumping to the side to keep from being run over.

Jack got back in the car as the bus disappeared around a curve. Twice now, he had seen captive Americans, and both times, almost in front of his eyes, they had disappeared. Was he imagining all of this? Had he underestimated the stress of revisiting the places that had scarred his mind and body so many years ago? Had he finally lost control?

No. He knew what he saw.

Jack no longer wanted to see O'Donnell or Cabanatuan. He had more important things to do. When he and Charlie had sat across the road from the little house while the Japanese soldiers had savaged the Filipino girl, Charlie had said, "Someday, these sonsabitches are gonna pay for this." He knew now he couldn't free any of the prisoners. Somehow they would thwart his every effort like they had already done. But there was something he could do. As Charlie had vowed, he could make the Japanese pay for what they had done. He could get revenge for Charlie, Capt. Clark, Dick, Bobby, Malloy. For him, the war had started all over again.

CHAPTER 20

A travel agency in the hotel lobby made his airline and hotel reservations and, after filling out some routine paperwork, a visa to enter Japan was easily obtained from the Japanese embassy in Manila.

Sitting in his darkened hotel room the night before his departure for Tokyo, Jack formulated his plan. He would go to Japan and seek out the men who could have been responsible for the suffering and deaths of his friends and the thousands of other American prisoners. They could be easily identified. Japan had committed almost its entire male population to fight in World War II and any Japanese man 60 years or older would have surely served during the war. When he found one, he would deal with him like the Japanese had dealt with their prisoners on Bataan. The war crimes trials held after the war brought the leaders like Tojo to justice, but what of the others? The ones who'd actually killed and tortured.

Japan Air Line flight 1401 bound for Tokyo departed Manila on schedule. Jack had been one of the first passengers to board and a Japanese man sat next to him. Jack studied the man's face as he took his seat. There was nothing in the man's look to tell what he was thinking...hatred, resentment, contempt? The term *inscrutable* exactly described the expression of Orientals because you could never tell what they thinking. But perhaps that was the best way to be. Jack was sure hatred was visible on his own face and might betray his intentions. He must not show his emotions. The man was middle aged, well-dressed and sat straight up in his seat, tightly clutching a leather briefcase in his lap. Most passengers had put their carry-on baggage in the overhead bins or under their seats, but the man next to Jack acted as if his briefcase held something so valuable that it couldn't be allowed out of his sight. He would love to snatch it from the man, tear it open, and see what it contained. He imagined all sorts of things...large sums of money, confidential business papers, state secrets...or maybe government lists of Americans still being held by the Japanese.

The busy Haneda Airport was teeming with people of every nationality. After claiming his luggage and clearing customs, Jack hailed a taxi for the trip to the Sanyo Hotel in the heart of Tokyo. Careening through the crowded streets like a mad man, the driver narrowly avoided one collision after another, one time slamming on his brakes so violently that Jack was almost thrown completely out of his seat. Jack marveled at how, when it appeared they would hit another car, the taxi would veer away as if one vehicle had a positive charge and the other negative, repelling each other when they got close.

The Sanyo was located just blocks from the glittery, upscale Ginza, known for its department stores, boutiques, restaurants, bars, and nightclubs. As Jack stood at his window watching the people scurrying along the busy street he formulated his plan of revenge. First he had to have a weapon, but not just any weapon. It had to meet a carefully defined criteria. It had to be easy to obtain with no questions asked. It had to be easy to conceal. It had to be deadly. And most important of all, it had to cause the victim to suffer for as long as possible before he died. He wanted them to suffer the way Malloy and Clark had suffered. He wanted to see them suffer like the men at O'Donnell and Cabanatuan suffered. A gun was definitely out. Guns were hard to obtain and not even all policemen carried them. Moreover a gun would attract unwanted attention. A garrote was a possibility but that would have to be done from behind and he wanted to see their face as they died. He wanted to see fear in their eyes when they faced certain death, like he had seen in Larry's eyes as he knelt awaiting execution by the sword wielding guard. He wanted a weapon that would cause a lingering death. Silent and deadly.

On the ride from the airport Jack had paid little attention to the weather but now as he emerged from the Sanyo he shivered in the damp, cold air. Most of the men on the street wore long, black overcoats. His light suit was suitable for the Philippines but not here. He needed a long, black overcoat. It would keep him warm, make him less conspicuous, and allow him to conceal a weapon.

Entering a large department store, he found the coat department and began to search through the assortment of black coats to find one that fit. Most were made for shorter Japanese men, and all he tried on would strike him above the knees. A clerk, seeing his problem, approached and nodded his head in understanding. With a bow, he turned and disappeared through the door to the stock room. Several minutes later, he returned with a black cashmere that was a perfect fit. Jack put the coat on and then bought an expensive black felt hat. With the collar turned up, and the brim of the hat pulled low, he looked, except for his height, like an ordinary Japanese businessman. And the height didn't worry him...there were some tall Japanese; He'd seen one at the warehouse door in San Fernando.

After Jack left the department store he walked the streets making mental notes of street names, restaurants, and stores. On a side street, a window display caught his attention. On a black lacquer stand were several Samurai swords much like the one the Japanese officer at Cabanatuan had swung with such deadly precision. Jack stood staring at the gleaming blades for several minutes before entering the store.

The store was a virtual step back in time. The walls were lined with Samura*i* dress and helmets, paintings of Samurai figures in battle, and literally hundreds of Samurai swords and daggers of every size and description. A wizened old man with a wispy beard sat on a stool at the rear of the store and watched as Jack slowly studied the many weapons that covered the walls.

One particular dagger caught his eye. It was beautifully crafted with an inch-wide blade. When he ran his finger lightly along the gleaming blade, he felt a sting and a thin red line of blood appeared on the skin.

The handle was wrapped with leather binding, making it easy to grip and, more important, fingerprints would be impossible to detect. He had found his weapon. Taking the dagger from its place on the wall Jack went to the rear of the store.

"I want to buy. How much?"

The old man turned his head toward a door at the back of the store and said something in Japanese. Instantly, a young man parted the curtain of wooden beads that hung to the floor.

"May I help you?" he said.

"Yes, thank you. I would like to purchase this dagger. Could you tell me how much it costs?"

"The price is 11,000 Yen."

Jack calculated in his mind. At the present exchange rate, that would be around $300.

"That is very expensive for just a small dagger."

The young man smiled. "Yes, but this is not just a dagger. This is an authentic *tanto,* a Samurai dagger. I have the provenance showing it was made in the 17th Century for a Samurai warrior and passed through the years to his descendants. One of those descendants was a military officer during World War II who used it to commit Seppuku."

Jack repeated, "Seppuku?"

"You might know it as Hara-Kiri. The officer is said to have committed Hara-Kiri after his command was defeated by the Americans."

Jack turned the dagger over and over in his hand, feeling its razor edge, sharp point, and perfect balance. Studying the weapon, he visualized in his mind the Japanese officer plunging the sharp point into his abdomen.

"This is just what I want."

As the young man put the dagger in a box, Jack complimented him on his English.

"I was afraid when I came to Tokyo that I wouldn't be able to communicate with people, but your English is excellent."

"That is because I'm young. If you have trouble finding someone to speak English, always find a young person. Children are taught English from the first grade on."

Looking at the old man. "My grandfather knows no English. They didn't teach English to school children when he was young."

"How old is your grandfather?"

"He is 95."

Jack thought briefly about the old man in the store being his first choice for retribution. How ironic for his first victim to have sold his executioner the instrument for his own destruction? But at 95, he would've been too old to have been in the war.

As he took the box and turned to leave, the young man said, "I hope you enjoy it."

A faint smiled played across Jacks face. "More than you'll ever know."

When he returned to his room, he removed the dagger from its box and sat staring at the gleaming blade. The young clerk's words played through his mind again and again: "The officer is said to have committed Hara-Kiri." That's how he would do it. Thrust it into the abdomen and then rotate the blade to destroy the internal organs. It was perfect. *Silent and deadly.*

Standing before a mirror, Jack put on his new coat and tried various ways to conceal and then quickly draw the dagger. The 11 inch blade was too long to fit in the pocket. Sticking it through his belt restricted his movement. Then he remembered a movie where a gangster had tied a cord around the butt of a sawed-off shotgun, looped the cord over his shoulder, and let the gun hang down his side underneath his coat. Jack cut one of his shirts into several strips, knotted them together and made a loop from which to hang the dagger. With his coat on no one could detect the deadly weapon. With a few minutes of practice, he was able to reach into his unbuttoned coat, grasp the hilt, and bring the blade out with a forward thrusting motion. *Silent and deadly.*

CHAPTER 21

Jack awoke still fully clothed. He had lain back across the bed, his hand resting lightly on the dagger and thought of Mary and the wonderful years they'd spent together. He could see her in her starched white uniform as she stood by his bed during those dark days at Letterman. For hours, deep into the night, memories of their life together played endlessly through his mind until he finally fell asleep.

After a leisurely lunch in the hotel's western style restaurant, he bought a *New York Times* and sat in his room reading the paper until the afternoon light began to fade. Standing in front of a mirror, Jack carefully hung the dagger over his right shoulder, put the coat on and pulled the hat low on his forehead to shade his eyes. The bulky coat made him look heavier then he was and, when he turned up the collar and slouched his shoulders he looked shorter than his 6'3".

It was time.

The sidewalks outside the Sanyo were crowded. Young professionals, their heads bowed against the icy wind, rushed home from work. The stream of people flowed around him like a swiftly moving river rushing around a boulder. His adrenaline surged as he felt the cold blade of the dagger nestled down his side.

Several times he saw men who fit the profile he had developed for his victims, but each time they would be swallowed by the crowds. Standing with his back to a glass storefront, Jack watched the people go by. Then he saw him. The man appeared to be 60 to 65 years old. He walked with a slight limp and had a jagged scar that started at the left corner of his mouth and ran almost to the ear. Jack had no doubt this man had fought in the war. The age was right. The limp, the scar had to be relics of some long-ago battle. Jack moved into the crowd, shadowing his prey. He wouldn't lose this one.

At the end of the block, the man descended stairs that led to the subway. As he watched, the man deposited a token and passed through the turnstile before disappearing down the loading platform. Jack rushed to the token booth, pushing ahead of a woman already in line, and thrust a 1000-yen note through the window. Without waiting for his change, he scooped up the tokens and rushed through the turnstile. As he elbowed his way through the crowded platform, he saw him again standing in front of a large, color-coded map of the subway system. Pretending to study the map, Jack was able to get a better look at his victim. As he furtively watched the man all doubts as to whether he was a former member of the Japanese army were erased... crew-cut gray hair, scar, an erect military bearing. Jack was sure he had been career military, probably an officer. One time he turned and looked in Jack's direction, and he had the uncomfortable feeling that the man somehow realized he was being stalked.

While waiting, Jack looked at the map more closely. It was a maze of red, blue, yellow, and green lines depicting the vast Tokyo subway system but surprisingly easy to understand. They were in the Ginza Station on the red line and he was certain he could find his way back to the hotel. He didn't want to get lost and have to ask questions that might draw attention to himself. Although he didn't consider what he was about to do a crime, he knew the police would. They would see him as a criminal rather than a soldier still fighting the war. He would have to be careful. He couldn't take the chance of wandering around a neighborhood or stopping people on the street to ask questions. He would have to move swiftly. Like guerrilla warfare-find the enemy, move in with lightning speed, strike, then out before the enemy knew what hit him.

The train glided noiselessly to a stop behind him, and Jack was startled when the scar-faced man stepped forward, almost brushing against him as he headed for the open door. Jack rushed to get through the door before it closed. Keeping the man in sight, Jack moved to the far end of the crowded car near a second door. He wanted to be able to leave the train at the same time without his victim knowing he was being followed.

At each stop, Jack would edge toward the door in case the man suddenly got off. At the fifth stop, the man stepped through the door…AKASKA Station. Jack waited for the man to reach the top of the stairs before he started up taking two steps at a time. When he emerged at street level, it was dark but he could see the man limping down a street lined with small, neat houses. As he disappeared around a corner, Jack broke into a trot fearing the man would disappear into a house before he could reach the corner. Jack slowed to a walk when a person walking in the opposite direction turned and looked at him. This was no time to attract unwanted attention. When Jack turned the corner, the man was still in sight. Midway down the block the man entered a house with a green door.

Standing in the shadows across the narrow street Jack watched the house the man had entered. He knew he must act quickly or arouse suspicion on the nearly empty street. But first he had to steel himself to the task. He had never killed a man at close range. He had shot at the enemy during the battles on Bataan, but this would be different. He would be up close...actually pressing against the body as he drove the dagger into the stomach. Killing couldn't be more personal than this. Just the thought was exhilarating.

Crossing the street in long strides, Jack knocked loudly on the green door. He had unbuttoned his coat as he strode toward the house and now gripped the dagger. At first there was only silence from the other side of the door. Then as Jack was raising his hand to knock again, the door opened and the man with the scar stood directly in front of him. In one swift motion Jack reached out, clasped his hand over the mouth, pushed him back against the door and thrust the dagger deep into the abdomen. Jack could feel a surge of air as a muffled scream pushed against his hand. Staring into the terrified eyes, he slowly rotated the handle so that the sharp blade would cut through the organs. The man's eyes were open as he slid down the door and there was a gurgling sound as blood from his mutilated intestines welled up into the throat. Jack pulled out the dagger, wiping the blade on the man's shirt. Then, using the victims blood Jack wrote on the door in big, bold letters *"MALLOY"* and under that, the numbers *"201."*

The collar of his coat turned up and the hat brim pulled low, Jack hurried back to the Akaska subway station. No one seemed to notice the tall man walking rapidly past the small houses.

It took him no more than five minutes to reach the loading platform, and a train going in the direction of the Ginza station arrived almost immediately. The train, inbound to the business district, was less crowded than earlier and he easily found a seat at the rear of the car. His heart still raced from the excitement, and sitting slouched in his seat he played the whole thing again in his mind. It had gone just as planned. He would never forget the look in the doomed man's eyes and he wondered if his victim had seen the same look in the eyes of the young American soldiers he had most certainly killed those many years ago.

When he reached his room at the Sanyo, Jack washed all traces of blood from the dagger and placed it under the shirts in his suitcase. Removing his clothes, he inspected them carefully for any traces of blood and finding none started the water for a hot shower before settling down on the soft bed.

* * *

During the final days as Chief of Detectives, Kenji would open the center drawer of his desk each morning, take out a small calendar, and put a red X on the day's date-It was his way of keeping track of the days left until retirement. As he marked the calendar, he counted 21 days. Three short weeks and he could start the next phase of his life. He had enjoyed his job, but it was time to move on.

The record of the Detective Bureau since he had been its chief was unparalleled in the history of The Tokyo Metropolitan Prefecture. In the past three years, more than 95% of the crimes committed in the city had been solved. His men were so good at what they did, they required little supervision and his job had become almost boring. This morning, however, as he looked through the report from the preceding evening, one crime caught his attention.

He pressed the button on the intercom that connected him with his deputy chief. "Watanabe-San, please come to my office." The door swung open so quickly that Kenji thought Watanabe must have been waiting to be called.

Watanabe was always up on everything so Kenji knew the answer before he asked. "Are you familiar with the murder in the Akaska District?"

"Yes sir."

Kenji motioned Watanabe to a chair. "It's very unusual to have a murder in that area. Could you please brief me on it?"

"The victim was an accountant named Hamada who worked for Sony and was nearing retirement. His wife said he had just arrived home from work and she was preparing their dinner when there was a knock on the door. He left to answer it and when he didn't return to the dining area after 10 or 15 minutes, she went to investigate and found him lying in the open door. There was a small amount of blood on his shirt and blood coming from his mouth."

"Wasn't that a long time to wait before she checked on him?" Kenji asked.

"I know what you're thinking Tanaka-san but I don't consider the wife a suspect."

"Oh? And why is that?" Kenji asked.

"The first officers arrived soon after the murder and found no weapon during a thorough search of the premises and surrounding area. It would have been impossible for the wife to dispose of the weapon in so short a time," Watanabe explained.

Kenji considered his deputy one of the finest detectives he had ever known. Watanabe could look a suspect in the face and immediately know whether the person was guilty or innocent. He was very seldom wrong.

"Please proceed."

"Hamada-san was killed by a single stab wound to the abdomen."

"Has an autopsy been performed?"

"I should have the results shortly."

"Motive? Evidence of robbery? Known connections to a criminal element? Financial problems?"

"None that have been determined but it's still early in the investigation."

"Any witnesses?"

"A tall man was seen running down the street but the witness couldn't provide a good description."

"A *tall* man?"

"Yes sir. But we're not sure if this is a significant lead. The man was running toward the victim's house rather than away."

"Do any 'tall men' live in or frequent that neighborhood?"

"None that we have found."

"That could be a significant lead if there are no 'tall men' commonly seen in that neighborhood."

"Yes sir. We will pursue it further."

Kenji, had the feeling that his deputy had not told him everything and was troubled by some aspect of this case. He prodded for more information.

"Is there something else?"

"Something very puzzling," said Watanabe. "Written in blood on the victim's door were the English letters 'M A L L O Y' and under that the numerals '2-0-1.'"

Eyebrows raised in surprise. "Malloy?"

"Yes sir and the numerals '2-0-1.'"

Something stirred in Kenji's mind. Those numbers meant something to him but whatever it was stayed just out of reach in the depths of his memory.

"I have been well schooled in the English language," Kenji said, "but I'm not familiar with that word. Why would an English word be written in the victim's blood? And what could be the significance of the numerals? Talk to your friend at the American Embassy to see if he can help us with that…and please show me the autopsy report as soon as you receive it."

* * *

Sitting up on the edge of the bed, Jack looked at his watch. He had slept soundly for ten hours, his best night's sleep since leaving home. Sliding his feet into his slippers he went to the window and looked down at the crowded street. Cars inched down the street and the sidewalks teemed with the citizens of Tokyo hurrying about their business.

Refreshed from his good night's sleep, Jack dressed hurriedly and went down to the hotel coffee shop for a late breakfast. As he strolled through the lobby, Jack noticed a newspaper rack displaying a Japanese language newspaper. Staring at the incomprehensible print he wondered if it contained news of what the police were probably calling "a brutal, senseless murder." If they only knew. Brutal? Yes, probably so. But no more brutal than what the Japanese guards had done on the Death March. Not as brutal as the beheading of the ten men at Cabanatuan. Senseless? Definitely not. It made perfect sense. These people must be punished for the crimes they committed on Bataan.

Leaving the hotel, Jack mingled with the people on the crowded sidewalk. Several times he saw men who fit his intended victims' profile, but each time he would be thwarted when they would enter a building or drive away in a car. One man in particular caught his attention because he so much resembled the Japanese officer who had Lt. Carson dragged away at Mariveles. It had been years since that day, but that face, like so many others, was burned into his memory. Jack followed the man until he entered a small tearoom and took a seat at a small table. Jack watched through the window as the man sipped from a cup of steaming tea. Suddenly, as if the man felt his stare, he turned and looked directly at Jack. Jack quickly turned away. Moments later when he looked through the window again, the man had disappeared. Jack scanned the faces in the small room but the man was gone. Had he unwittingly done something to warn the man of the danger he was in? He must be more discreet in his hunt for the next victim.

Jack could feel the cold steel of the dagger against his ribs as he wandered the streets searching for his next victim. He had been so focused on finding a victim that he was surprised when he realized that the sun had sunk below the horizon and looming above was the Tokyo Tower. He was in an industrial district and the street was deserted except for a man walking toward him on the opposite side of the street. The only light came from the brightly lit tower, but it was enough for Jack to know that he had found his next victim. He angled across the street to intercept the man near a space between two buildings. The man who had been walking head down, eyes on the ground looked up as Jack drew near. Even though the man couldn't know he had only minutes to live, fear was etched on the weathered face...just what Jack wanted to see. He wanted him to feel the same fear that he and Charlie had felt during those dark days as prisoners of the Japanese.

The man, sensing the impending danger turned away just as Jack reached him. Jack reached out and coiled an arm tightly around the man's neck. Dragging him into the narrow space between the buildings, Jack spun the little man around and drove the dagger deep into the abdomen, working it from side to side, then up and down. A high pitched scream turned to a gurgle as blood welled up in the dying man's throat.

"This is for Charlie," Jack said as he let the man's limp body slide to the ground.

* * *

The autopsy report on the Hamada killing was pretty much as Kenji had expected, except for one thing. The medical examiner had said that after the dagger had been thrust into the abdomen, the blade had been rotated to slice through the internal organs. It had been a slow, agonizing death as the heart pumped all of the blood into the mutilated cavity. No doubt the man had suffered greatly. It had been a particularly vicious attack and, since no valuables had been taken, Kenji could only assume that this had been an act of hate...or revenge. But who could hate this mild-mannered accountant *that much?*

For the past 24 hours, Watanabe and his detectives had interrogated family, neighbors, friends, and fellow workers and, as far as they could ascertain, Hamada had been a peaceful man with no known enemies. He had a happy marriage, a modest income, lived in a modest house and was well liked by everyone who knew him. Sixty-eight years old, he had been injured in an industrial accident as a young man that left him with a jagged scar on his face and a crippled leg, exempting him from service during World War II. He had spent the war years working in a munitions factory in Osaka then had returned to school and learned accounting. For over 20 years he had been an excellent employee for Sony and was looking forward to his retirement at the end of the year.

Watanabe's friend in the American Embassy was Tom McGee, a former FBI agent who was now the embassy's Chief of Security. The United States invited police officers from other countries to attend the FBI Academy, and Watanabe had gone there for specialized training. The academy was located in Virginia, and during free time, Watanabe had been able to visit Washington, D.C., and the surrounding area. It had been an enlightening experience. He had not only learned the latest crime-solving technology but had also developed great respect for his country's former enemy. Tom McGee was an instructor of investigative techniques and, when he retired from the FBI, came to Tokyo and promptly looked up his former student. When Watanabe told Tom what had been written in the victim's blood, the former agent knew that the killer had written an American name.

From his office window, Kenji stared out over the city and tried to comprehend why an American name would be scrawled on the door of a murder victim in Tokyo, Japan. And what could the numerals 201 mean? It made no sense. And that was why this case troubled him so. It made no sense. If you looked closely enough and long enough, you could usually find a reason for every murder but he had the uneasy feeling that the motive for this killing would be much more complex than any other he had worked on.

Kenji turned toward the door as Watanabe rushed in. "A call just came in. Another stabbing victim has been found! Sounds very similar to the Hamada case."

Kenji opened his desk drawer and removed the revolver. "I'll go with you."

It was a short distance from The Government Building to the narrow space between two buildings near the Tokyo Tower. Like Hamada, the elderly man had a single stab wound in the abdomen and Kenji had no doubt what the autopsy report would say. And just like before, scrawled on the concrete wall in the victim's blood was a word and once again the numbers 201. The letters, left in a large, bloody scrawl were C-H-A-R L-I-E...Charlie. Kenji knew this too was an American name. Two American names left at the murder scenes, and the same numerals...201. Again, something stirred in the recesses of his mind-somewhere in his past, those numbers had meant something important to him.

With a sinking heart, Kenji realized that a madman was roaming the streets of Tokyo killing Japanese men, and he had no clue of who it was or how to stop him.

* * *

CHAPTER 22

Jack pulled open the curtains and the bright afternoon sun flooded the room. He had gotten careless the night before. After leaving the man lying between the buildings, he had attempted to retrace his steps back to the hotel but he had not paid enough attention to where he was going as he searched the streets for his next victim. By midnight, he was hopelessly lost and hailed a passing taxi, giving the driver the name of a restaurant several blocks from the hotel. He had to be more careful. If the police learned a taxi had picked up a man near the murder scene, they might be able to track him down. He couldn't be that careless again. A map was the answer.

The next morning he found just what he needed at a small sidewalk kiosk...a tourist map showing subway routes, major buildings and the sightseeing attractions throughout the city. Spreading the map out on the desk in his room, he found the location of the first killing by following the subway line from the Ginza station to the Akaska station. When he was certain he had the exact location of the house with the green door, he took his ballpoint and marked it with a circled X. The second was more difficult. All he could go by was the location of he Tokyo Tower that had loomed above. After studying the area around the tower for some time, he placed another circled X where the second man had paid for his crimes against him and his friends.

* * *

Kenji was just two weeks from retirement, but he had no intention of leaving until the killer was apprehended. He had already talked to his superiors and they agreed that he could remain at his job for an indefinite period, but he knew their patience would grow thin if the killer wasn't brought to justice soon.

He had assigned five detectives to the first killing and another five more to the latest killing. The men working the Hamada case had literally worked around the clock but were no closer to solving the killing than they had been at the beginning.

He was sure of only one thing...the same person had committed both murders. But why had the killer chosen such disparate individuals? Hamada was a respected family man who had worked for the same company for many years. Mashita, the second victim, was a common laborer with a long record of petty crimes. What could possibly link these two men?

When they left the site of where the second victim was found Kenji and Watanabe returned to the site of the Hamada killing. Standing across the narrow street from the green door Kenji wondered why the killer had chosen that particular door to knock on? How could it be completely random? The killer must have known that his victim was home and would open the door in response to his knock. No one had seen a car near the house around the time of the murder, so it stood to reason that the killer was on foot. And since no one saw anyone loitering on the street the killer had probably followed his victim home. That would mean the killer had ridden the subway from the Ginza district just as Hamada had. Was he the "tall man" seen running? Kenji had the chilling thought that Hamada had seen his killer on the train, maybe even spoken to him.

Sending his driver back to headquarters, Kenki walked from the Akaska station to Hamada's house. It took barely five minutes. Hamada's wife stated her husband had arrived home promptly at 6:20 p.m. just as he had every day for the last 20 years. That meant the train carrying the fateful duo arrived at the Akaska station at 6:15. He would tell Watanabe to locate other people who had ridden that particular train to see if any could remember the two men who had gotten off. The same people rode that train every day on their way home from work, day in and day out, and perhaps someone had noticed a stranger...a tall stranger.

When Kenji returned to his office, he told Watanabe to assemble the detectives working on the two cases for a meeting. Promptly at 4, the ten detectives followed by Watanabe filed into the briefing room. After they had taken their seats, Chief of Detectives Kenji Tanaka entered and went to the podium. His confidence grew as he looked out at the men. They were the best he had and he would put them up against anyone.

"All right, let's get started."

The chatter died as Kenji shuffled the papers in front of him.

"As all of you know, a second victim has been found and it appears that both victims were killed by the same person or persons. A citizen going to work near the tower found the body lying in a narrow space between two buildings. The medical examiner put the time of death as between 7 and 10 P.M. the preceding evening. The victim, a 65-year-old man named Mashita, was killed with a knife or possibly a short sword that was thrust in the abdomen and then rotated, mutilating the internal organs. This is a slow, particularly painful death in which the victim bleeds to death internally."

After a brief pause, Kenji continued. "As before, a word was written in the victim's blood. It was written in English and the letters were 'C-H-A-R-L-I-E', an American name. Below that were the English numerals '201'. We are faced with a crisis and, unless we can stop the killer, we will find many more bodies. Now let's hear your theories, possible motives, or just plain guesses."

A hand shot up in the back of the room, a detective assigned to the Hamada case. "This may sound crazy," he said, but the way the knife is used is the same way that the knife is used in the Hara-Kiri ritual."

Kenji nodded. "A good observation but if the killer is attempting to emulate the hara-kiri ritual, he has failed miserably. Hara-kiri, as practiced by the Samurai, was an act of honor. The way these men have been killed appears to be designed to degrade, dehumanize and cause great pain. But that's the kind of ideas we need. Say anything that comes to mind. You never know what might make sense when we start to tie things together. What else?"

Another hand went up.

"Since no valuables appear to have been taken, we need to consider whether these are crimes of hatred or revenge."

"A strong possibility," said Kenji.

Turning to a large blackboard behind the podium, he printed in capital letters "MOTIVE" and in two columns below that the words "HATRED" and "REVENGE."

"What else?"

An older detective spoke up. "Since American names were found at the murder scenes, I believe the killer is an American."

"Those could also be British names," another added.

Kenji turned to the board and made another column titled "SUSPECTS" and under that, "AMERICAN" and "BRITISH."

Turning back to face the group, "Have we been able to establish any connection between the two victims?"

This time, Watanabe spoke. "Only one."

"And that is?"

"Perhaps I should have said two. They were both males between 65 and 70."

Once again turning to the blackboard, he drew another column, labeling it "VICTIMS," and under that, "Males 65-70."

"Any other connection?"

"None that we have been able to find," Watanabe said.

"Watanabe-san has made an excellent connection concerning the age of the victims. But what does that tells us?"

A detective named Konishi spoke up. "Perhaps he hates older men for some reason."

"Like his father," another added.

"Or a tyrannical boss."

"Perhaps, but if we think the killer is American, why would he come to Japan to kill Japanese men when he hates an American father? And as for a tyrannical boss, would he not kill the boss instead of two men he doesn't even know? But anything is a possibility and we will keep it under consideration." Kenji wrote to the side of "hatred" in the motive column, "Father figure/Boss."

"Anyone else? No? Then let me tell you what I think. I, too, think the killer is probably an American. First there's the matter of American names and numerals found at the scene and one other clue that has been largely over-looked…the tall man seen running down the sidewalk near the victim's home. We've determined no tall men live in that area. In fact, with one notable exception, there aren't that many tall Japanese men."

Kenji paused to let the laughter subside after the obvious reference to his unusual height.

A detective near the back of the room held up his hand. "But the 'tall man' was seen running towards Hamadas' house not away."

"Perhaps there is an explanation for that. Can anyone tell us what this reason could be?"

Receiving no response, Kenji said, "Then let me give you a possible reason. There were no suspicious vehicles in the area and I believe the killer followed Hamada from the subway. When he saw him turn the corner, it's possible he was running so as not to lose sight of him."

Seeing nods of understanding, Kenji continued," And then we have the Mashita case. Any theories on it?"

A young detective that Kenji believed showed great promise as a detective raised his hand. "I have an observation on the locations."

Kenji nodded to the man. "Please let us hear your observation."

"The two killings were almost five kilometers apart on a direct east-west axis. I would think that a man on foot, like we believe might be the case, would reside somewhere in between the two murder sites. If you pick the exact midpoint, two and a half kilometers east of the first and two and a half west of the second, you are in the heart of the Ginza."

"Excellent. A vital observation. This would seem to confirm that the killer rode the subway from the Ginza station just as Hamada did."

"If the killer is an American staying in the Ginza," Watanabe said, "he must be choosing his victims randomly."

"But maybe they meet a certain criteria. I have thought for many hours what connection the two victims could have. My conclusion is World War II. If this is correct, then I believe the killer would be of a similar age as the victims and would have fought in the Pacific during the war. This person could have developed a great hatred of Japanese men because of some experience he had in the war. War can do that to a man."

Konishi spoke again. "But the war ended over 40 years ago."

"That is correct but I recently attended a lecture given by Dr. Hiwakawa on Post-Traumatic Stress Disorder. A mental imbalance can occur in some people who have suffered a very traumatic experience. The killer could have been traumatized by his wartime experiences but was able to cope, perhaps with the aid of doctors or loved ones, until another traumatic event triggered all of his pent up anger.

"This theory may or may not be correct, but we need a starting point and, until we have something better, this will be our focus. We are going to look for an American who is at least 60 years old, a recent arrival in our country, who fought in the Pacific during the war and who suffered a recent traumatic event in his life. We will work on the assumption that this American is staying at a hotel in the Ginza."

Watanabe-san, assemble teams to canvas all hotels in or near the Ginza for Americans who fit this description. Discount no American, but we will investigate more thoroughly those who fit the criteria I have outlined. It will be time consuming but not impossible."

As the men filed out, Kenji wondered how many more would die before they could complete the task.

* * *

Jack was sure the police were searching for the killer of the two men they had found in the last few days, but when he left the hotel just before dark and saw a police cruiser driving slowly down the street with two officers scrutinizing the crowded sidewalk, he never suspected they were looking for him. Nonetheless he instinctively turned away and pretended to show interest in a store window display. In the glass he saw the cruiser pass and then stop. The officers got out and approached two men on the sidewalk. From a distance Jack couldn't be certain but they didn't look oriental. The officers talked to the men for several minutes and when they took wallets from their pockets it was apparent they had been asked for identification. The officers made notes on a pad and then returned to their cruiser. When they were out of sight, Jack hurried to catch up with the two men. When he was close enough to overhear their conversation, he knew they were Americans..

"Excuse me," he said.

The men stopped and turned.

"Hello, I just arrived here and saw the police stop you. Were they asking for passports? I left mine in the hotel and didn't know if I needed to carry it with me all the time. I certainly don't want to break the law."

The older of the two, who looked to be in his late forties, smiled. "They just wanted to see some I.D."

"What did they write down?"

"Our names, our age and where we are staying," said the younger man.

"Is that something they do here often?" Jack asked.

The older of the two spoke again. "I've been coming here about four times a year for the last 10 years and this is the first time it's ever happened."

"Did they say why they were doing it?"

"No, but I know a little Japanese and I think I heard one of them say something about being too young...I definitely heard the word killer."

As Jack walked away, his mind reeled with what he had just seen and heard. The police were targeting Americans... an older American...in their search for a killer. Could they possibly know whom to look for? Had they connected the names *Malloy* and *Charlie* to an American? Writing their names may have been foolish, but he wanted these evil people to know why they were dying. To be looking for an *older* American was impressive detective work, but it didn't bother Jack...it added an element of excitement. Before it had only been him against his hapless victims, now he must also match wits against a worthy adversary.

* * *

After the meeting with Tanaka, Watanabe sent teams of detectives and uniformed officer to scour hotels for Americans registered as guests and who had been in the city during the times of the killings. By noon he had received another 20 uniformed officers to help in the search.

In the first six hours, a list of 53 men who fit the killers profile was compiled. Hotel employees were questioned concerning the Americans' probable ages and if they had observed anything that would arouse suspicion. Most were younger businessmen, but those that fit the age of the killer were placed under constant surveillance. Watanabe rushed the list of names to the American Embassy. McGee had agreed to send the names to the United States Justice and State Departments where records could be checked for pertinent information about the men, including age and military records. Maybe the age similarity of the victims was just a coincidence and they were wasting valuable time on an incorrect theory. He had great respect for his chief, but the possibilities were endless as to who was committing these horrible murders.

* * *

Jack returned to his room and sat in the semi-dark thinking about what he had learned. The police were looking for an "older" American. He wondered how many "older" Americans there were in Tokyo. From what he had seen here in the hotel and on the streets, probably not many. Most Americans he had seen, like the two on the street, were younger businessmen or servicemen stationed at nearby American bases. He knew this put him at a greater risk of being detected but he had a mission and like any good soldier he wouldn't abandon his mission because there was danger involved.

Jack left the Sanyo a little after 9 p.m. His first victims had been chosen completely at random from the Tokyo streets. This time he already knew who his victim would be…a street vendor selling steaming bowls of Soba. Short, bowed-legged, with muscular arms and broad shoulders, he looked like many of the Japanese guards he had seen during his years in captivity. People seemed to know him well and would stand and talk as they ate the noodles he served. He stood at the same corner from noon until late every night. Jack had seen him pushing his cart away from the corner around ten p.m. Tonight he planned to follow him and if the location were right, the "Soba Man" would be the next to die in Jack's war.

With the pressure being applied by the police, Jack considered this safer than indiscriminately walking the streets looking for victims. He didn't fear the police, however he had an increasing respect for them. And that was good. If you don't respect your enemy, you get careless, make mistakes, then suffer defeats. That was what had happened before Pearl Harbor. Americans hadn't taken these little men seriously, and had paid heavily for it. He knew better now.

It took Jack only a few minutes to walk the six blocks to where the vendor set up business every day. As he turned the corner, he could see the short, stocky man starting to push his cart down the side street leading away from the busy intersection. It was incredible how fast the little man could push the cumbersome cart. Jack, with his long stride, could hardly keep the man in sight. After several blocks, Jack saw a police car in the intersection ahead. More cautious then before, Jack stepped behind the corner of a building then had to hurry to catch up with his fast-moving quarry.

Block after block, the "Soba Man" pushed his cart. Jack was amazed at how far he had to go each day to reach his corner. Finally, he turned down a dark, narrow street lined with small shops already shuttered for the night. The street was deserted except for the vendor and his cart. Stopping in front of a weathered wood gate in a stone wall that connected two darkened shops, the vendor took a key tied to a string around his neck, and removed a lock from the gate. Standing in the shadows, Jack watched the "Soba Man" disappear inside, then almost immediately come back out, lock the gate, and walk away. Jack waited until he was sure there was no one around, then crossed the street and stood before the wooden gate. The top of the wall was high, but Jack easily reached the top and pulled himself up. In the faint light, he could see the cart standing in the center of a small courtyard and several old signs leaning against the back wall. Lowering himself back to the sidewalk, he turned and began to retrace his steps back to the "Soba Mans" corner.

Tomorrow night he would be waiting.

* * *

The second day of canvassing hotels for Americans yielded an additional 34 names, which were once again rushed to the American Embassy. When they got through the entire day without finding a new victim, Kenji held the faint hope that maybe, just maybe, they would get lucky and have the results on the first set of names before there were more killings. He tried to convince himself that they were on the right track, but what if the killer wasn't some American with a deep grudge against the Japanese he had fought against during the war? Then what? He knew his theory on the killings was a long shot and that even Watanabe had doubts about it.

But he knew things Watanabe didn't know, had seen things Watanabe hadn't seen. The fighting during the war had been ferocious and bitter and there had been atrocities committed on both sides. What had happened in the Philippines in the early months of the war was something he and probably any American soldier who had been there would never forget.

Kenji was back at his desk by six a.m studying the investigative reports that had accumulated on the two killings. He wanted to make sure he hadn't missed anything. There were detailed autopsy reports complete with pictures and the examiner's drawings. There were crime scene photos and interviews with friends, relatives, co-workers. There was crime-scene evidence. There was, however, not the slightest clue as to the killer's motive or identity.

Shortly after noon, Watanabe called to say that Tom McGee had gotten back the first list of 53 names with the desired information and he was on his way to pick it up. Kenji would have the list before the next killing.

But he had no sooner placed the phone back on the receiver when it rang again. It was the duty watch commander.

"Tanaka-san, another body has been found."

Kenji took a deep breath and leaned back in his chair. "Like the others?"

"It looks like the same killer."

When Kenji arrived at the scene, the wooden gate was held open by a uniformed officer while two others knelt by the body lying inside the courtyard. They had been dispatched just before the watch commander had notified Kenji of the latest killing and had sped to the scene, arriving just minutes before.

As he walked through the gate, Kenji saw the Soba cart and leaning against it a white sign that had once been used to advertise a merchant's wares. On the blank, back side, the killer had used the victim's blood to leave his latest message: *"CLARK"* and under that once again, *"201."* But the killer had left something else this time. There was a bloody thumbprint on the sign.

As Kenji examined the print, he said, "You just made your first mistake...and I'm going to get you. That's a promise."

Rising, Kenji looked more closely at the cart and thought it looked familiar. As he leaned between the detectives for a better view of the body, he instantly recognized the victim. As a young patrol officer, Kenji had often stopped and talked to Suzuki. For more than 20 years he had been an icon on the streets of Tokyo, always taking the time to dispense his own brand of wisdom, as well as the steaming hot noodles, to the many who sought his advice on any matter that troubled them. A highly decorated war veteran who had survived the battles of Iwo Jima and Okinawa, he had told Kenji how he had sat and cried when he killed his first American soldier in battle. How had such a cruel fate befallen such a gentle man?

The medical examiner arrived and, after examining the body for several minutes, stood and said, "I would say that he was killed sometime between 10 o'clock last night and 6 o'clock this morning. I probably don't need to tell you the method the killer used. From all outward appearances, it's the same as before."

Kenji turned to a detective, "Who found the body?"

A detective motioned to someone outside the gate and a uniformed officer came in with a pretty young lady who worked at the shop adjoining the storage area.

"This is Yoshiko."

The girl was small and Kenji had to bend low to look in her face. Tears were rolling down her cheeks.

"Yoshiko, I'm told that you discovered the body. Could you tell me about it?" Kenji gently asked.

"As I walked by, I saw the gate was not locked. Suzuki-san always locked the gate. I looked to see if perhaps he was inside and saw his body."

"Did you see Suzuki-san or anyone else enter the courtyard?"

With her eyes lowered, Yoshiko shook her head in a silent no.

Kenji turned to the two detectives, "The killer must have followed him in last night."

As he stepped out of the closed area, he noticed black scuff marks on the outside of the wall.

"And then again maybe not," he said. "Konichi-san, see if you can climb over this wall."

Konichi was of average height for a Japanese man but could not jump high enough to grasp the top and pull himself up. It would take someone over 6 feet tall to scale the wall. Like the tall man seen running the night of the Akaska killing.

* * *

Back in the hotel around midnight, Jack was relieved to see the lobby empty. The desk clerk was absorbed in a magazine and never looked up as Jack crossed the lobby. Sure that the police hunt for him was intensifying, Jack decided to walk up the five flights so that the sound of the elevator wouldn't attract the clerk's attention.

Too keyed up to sleep, Jack sat at the desk studying the map. He had counted the blocks the Soba Man had pushed his cart when he left his corner and was able to accurately put a circle and an X at the location of the small court-yard. On the side of the map was a list of Tokyo attractions. He had seen it before but had paid little attention. Now, however, he read with interest about Ueno Park, a large area in the center of the city with a zoo, several lakes, museums, and numerous paths that wound through secluded areas. Ueno Park would be the perfect place to find his next victim. By now, people were probably being warned that a killer was stalking his victims at night and everyone would be cautious, but here was the opportunity to strike in broad daylight. A secluded area would afford the same protection as darkness…and finding a victim would be easier during the day when more people were out.

Before he turned out the lights, Jack circled Ueno Park with his ballpoint pen.

* * *

When Kenji returned to his office, Watanabe was waiting with the list of the first 53 American men they had been able to identify as staying at Ginza hotels. Driving back to his office, he had fervently hoped that the killer's name was on the list and that somehow the information McGee had been able to obtain about the men would enable them to identify the killer. Short of that, he knew they would have to interview each suspect, a process that would take time...time they didn't have. Time to allow the killer to strike again.

As Kenji settled behind his desk, Watanabe started to read the names and information they had about each man.

"Paul Ashmore, age 60, auto design specialist for Honda. Home Nashville, Tennessee. No military service."

Kenji jotted the name on a pad, putting an X mark by the name.

"Leon Martin, age 65, retired business man. Married. Military service World War II, European Theater. Home, Atlanta, Georgia."

"Why is this Martin in Tokyo?"

"The people at the hotel are not sure but he is accompanied by a lady, presumably his wife."

Kenji wrote Martin and beside it in capital letters "European Theater. Wife. Not a suspect. "

And so it went, name after name. When they had gone through 41 names, Kenji had only marked three names as possible suspects, and none had fought in the Pacific during the war.

After a short pause while his secretary brought them a small pot of green tea that she poured into delicate, flowered cups, Kenji said, "Twelve names to go. Let's get on with it."

Jack Collins, age 63, retired businessman. Military service, World War II, Pacific Theater. Prisoner of war."

Kenji sat straight up in his chair.

A prisoner of war….in the Pacific?

Watanabe lowered the paper and said, "There's more."

Kenji leaned forward across the desk. "Go on."

"The military unit Jack Collins served in was the 201st Artillery Regiment stationed in the Philippines."

The Philippines. POW. The 201st Regiment. The same numbers left at the murder scenes. Kenji stood abruptly, overturning his cup of tea.

"Where is this Collins staying?"

"The Sanyo."

CHAPTER 23

The winding path was lined with trees and bushes making Ueno Park the ideal place to attack his next victim. The trees completely shut out the bustling sights and sounds of the city and Jack could see why the park was a favorite spot for the people of Tokyo.

Since his arrival in Tokyo, the city had been blanketed by low clouds that daily spit pellets of sleet that stung his cheeks or large, wet flakes of snow that settled softly on his cashmere coat and felt hat. Today, however, the sun had finally broken through and although the temperature still hovered near freezing, many people in the park were enjoying a day away from the hustle and bustle of the city streets.

When Jack entered the park, there was a large open area, scattered with buildings, several religious shrines and a pagoda but as he walked deeper into the park, trees closed in on both sides of the path. In places, it was difficult to see more than a few feet into the dense undergrowth. Occasionally, side paths led to areas adorned with benches, fountains, and small shrines. He knew he would find his next victim in one of these small, secluded areas.

* * *

Kenji Tanaka was almost certain he had the killer. Jack Collins fit the profile of the killer perfectly. During the war he had been stationed in the Philippines and had been a prisoner of war. It was entirely possible that Collins had been on The Death March, as the Americans had labeled the movement of prisoners out of Bataan after the war. Many Americans had died. Many had been mistreated, and Kenji knew from his own observations that his countrymen had committed horrific atrocities. Could this be the reason for the hatred this man has harbored all these years? And why had it taken over 40 years for him to seek his vengeance? What event had triggered this deep-seated anger? And Collins was in the 201st Artillery...201...the numbers found at each killing. The final piece had fallen into place.

With two phone calls, Kenji assembled a small army of police to storm the Sanyo and capture Collins. He wanted to make sure the killer could not slip through their fingers. Men were stationed at every entrance, stairway and elevator.

Kenji, Watanabe, two detectives, and four uniformed officers moved quietly down the fifth floor hallway to Collin's room. The plan was to burst through the door and overpower him. Kenji had thought briefly of warrants but had decided that time was of the essence. Any delay in capturing Collins could provide the opportunity to escape. He would worry about the technicalities later.

With their guns drawn, Kenji stepped to one side and motioned for a burly officer to throw himself against the door. As the doorframe splintered, Kenji led the officers into the room, guns sweeping back and forth. They searched the bathroom, closets, even under the bed. The room was empty.

Kenji cursed at his miscalculation. It was three in the afternoon and he had been sure Collins would be in his room since he was a night stalker and the people at the desk hadn't seen him leave. Kenji immediately sent one of the officers to disperse the others from in front of the hotel, fearing Collins would flee if he saw the police cars and officers guarding the entrance.

As the detectives continued to search the room for anything that would definitely link Collins to the murders, Watanabe, leaning over the small desk at one side of the room, exclaimed, "Kenji-san."

Kenji strode across the room and saw a Tokyo map spread out on the desk.

"Look at this!" Watanabe pointed to a spot on the map circled with a ballpoint pen...the exact spot in Akaska where the first killing had occurred.

"And look." Kenji pointed to another circle. "Here's where we found Suzuki. And here's the one near the tower. Iincredible. He marks his kills like the tiger in the jungle."

"And what is this?" Watanabe asked pointing to the circles around Ueno Park. "What could this mean? There's been no killing in the park."

"Perhaps this is his next move. We need to go there immediately."

As they rushed out the door, Kenji thought, "You just made your second mistake...I've got you now."

As Konichi sped through the Tokyo traffic, Kenji, barked orders into the radio. Officers would surround Ueno Park, while others would comb every inch of the sprawling park. If Collins were here, he wouldn't escape this time.

As the car screeched to a stop in front of the south entrance, Kenji jumped out, directing officers in various directions.

"He's in here. I feel it," he said to Watanabe. "You go towards the zoo and I'll go this way," pointing to a path that led into the park's interior.

"Be alert. We must catch him now."

* * *

Jack had been in the park for almost an hour and was growing impatient that he hadn't spotted his next victim. He had seen older women, some younger women with children, and in one case an entire family but no one that he could target for his next victim.

Rounding a curve in the path, Jack saw a man walking towards him. As they passed, the man smiled and bowed slightly in Jack's direction. He was a distinguished looking man with a full head of silver-gray hair and walked with his head held high, arms swinging at his sides in a measured gait as if he were marching in a military parade. No doubt this man had been an officer in the Japanese army.

After the man passed, Jack turned and followed at a discreet distance, careful not to arouse suspicion. Coming to a fork in the path, he turned and followed a side path to the left. Jack had already been down this path and knew it ended at a secluded pond surrounded by dense foliage. There was no other way out. Several benches were situated around the pond, and under a wooden shed a small Shinto shrine stood in a space carved out of the foliage. Perfect, Jack thought. The man, like an unwary fly, was heading straight into the trap.

As Jack e entered the clearing, he saw the man, seemingly in some type of prayer, standing, bent slightly at the waist, in front of the shrine. Unaware of the danger he was in, the man stood silently with his eyes closed. For the first time, Jack had doubts about his deadly mission. The man was praying and something deep inside of Jack stirred. In the dismal warehouse in San Fernando when he too had looked death in the face, he had also prayed...*Yea, thou I walk through the valley of the shadow of death.* To kill a man while he prayed- no matter how evil he was or what he had done-was something he could not do.

Jack stood with the dagger poised until the man straightened and turned to face him. Startled to see someone standing so close behind, the man's eyes narrowed and his jaw muscles tightened when he saw the dagger.

Jack hesitated and then with one swift motion he thrust the dagger into the man's abdomen. The man reached out with both hands and grasped Jack's hand in a futile attempt to force Jack to withdraw the blade. As Jack rotated the handle, the man's grasp gradually loosened and he sank to his knees, then fell forward on his face.

Jack knelt, dipping his finger into the victim's blood and began to write on the smooth concrete path *BUSTE..*, but before he could add the last letter he heard the sound of someone running on the path behind him. The steps paused momentarily, then started again. The curve in the path prevented him from seeing anyone but he was certain the steps were getting closer. Pulling the dagger from his victim's abdomen Jack rose, and stepped behind the shrine. Watching through a small crack in the shrine's wooden shed, Jack saw a tall Japanese man come into the clearing and then cautiously circle the pond. He had only seen a Japanese man that tall one time before...at the warehouse door in San Fernando when the Japanese officer had deflected the bayonet aimed at his own chest. As he lay there, he swore he would never forget that face-and through the years the features had come to him over and over again. As Kenji stood directly in front of the shrine looking at the body, Jack was positive that he was once again looking at the face of the tall Japanese officer who had saved his life.

* * *

Kenji went down the concrete path at a run, slowing at times to scan the area for any sign that might alert him to the presence of the killer. When he came to a fork in the path, he hesitated momentarily trying to decide which way to go. He knew it was pure chance if he went in the correct direction, but this entire case been based on chance A killer seeking vengeance, choosing victims by chance. His deduction that the killer had been an American who had fought against the Japanese during the war. Some might call it good detective work but he knew it was pure chance. And then picking Collins out of the list and finding the evidence they needed in his hotel room. Partly solid reasoning, partly chance. And now, if he took the correct path and found Collins, it would be chance again.

Kenji slowed as he entered the clearing. It wasn't until he had walked halfway around the pond that he saw the body sprawled on the pavement in front of the shrine, blood still oozing coming from the victim's mouth. Kenji cursed silently as he realized he had just been moments too late to save the man.

Looking cautiously around Kenji saw and heard nothing. He bent over the body to read the bloody message that Collins had left. *BUSTE..* Another American name? But something was different this time. And then it dawned on him. The numbers 201 were missing. He must have interrupted the ritual Collins performed after every killing and that he might at this very moment be lurking nearby.

Kenji rose slowly, reaching for his gun. Hearing a noise behind him he turned quickly and saw a man step from behind the shrine holding a bloodstained dagger. As he stepped back, Kenji stumbled over the body, and fell backward. The gun slipped from his hand and clattered to the pavement. In four long strides, Collins was standing over him. Kenji braced himself, ready to roll to the side in an attempt to avoid the lethal blade.

But Collins just stood there.

Kenji, without taking his eyes from the menacing figure hovering over him, continued to feel around for his gun. Just as he found it, Collins reached out with his empty hand.

Kenji raised the gun and fired one shot.

* * *

EPILOGUE

When word got out that the killer stalking the streets of Tokyo was dead, congratulations began to pour in. Even the Prime Minister had called, calling Kenji a hero and telling him he would intervene to prevent his impending retirement if he desired. Kenji thanked the Prime Minister but politely declined his help in staying on the force.

As he and Watanabe sat discussing the case, Kenji said, "I'm still puzzled by Collin's behavior at the end. As I laid there helpless he could have killed me if he'd wanted to…but he didn't even try."

"That *is* peculiar."

"In fact when he reached out his hand, it was almost as if he intended to help me up. And…", Kenji's voice trailed off as he rose to put on his coat. "I'm very tired. Think I'll go home for a nice hot bath and dinner."

"You were going to say something else?"

"He was smiling when I shot him."

He wasn't sure why-morbid curiosity maybe-but one last time he wanted to see this man's body. Stopping at the medical examiner's office, he was told he could view the body in the lab where it was being readied for autopsy.

The body lay on a stainless steel table covered by a white sheet. As the medical examiner pulled back the sheet, Kenji's attention was riveted on the left arm, where just below a scarred shoulder was a beautiful red, white, and blue tattoo of an eagle, wings spread, clutching a bundle of arrows in its talons.

Suddenly, Kenji was transported back in time to 1942, watching American POW's being herded through the warehouse door at San Fernando. A young American soldier had turned and bolted back out the door, only to be knocked down by a guard's rifle butt. Then, he had instinctively reached out, deflecting the bayonet being thrust at the soldier's chest and the blade had torn into the fallen soldier's left shoulder instead. Another American knelt and tore away the sleeve that was emblazoned with...yes, he remembered now...the numbers 201. As the cloth was torn away, a tattoo had been revealed, the exact one he was looking at now. The scarred shoulder, the tattoo. This was the same man. He had thought of that tattoo many times, wondering what had happened to that American. Now he knew.

Kenji stood staring at the body as the truth of Jack Collin's last moments came into focus. As hard as it was to believe, Collins must have recognized him and couldn't kill the man who had saved his life so many years before. Kenji pulled the sheet over the pale, lifeless face.

The war had finally ended for Jack Collins.

Cowards die many times before their

deaths;

The valiant never taste of death but once.

Of all the wonders that I have yet heard,

It seems to me most strange that men

should fear;

Seeing that death, a necessary end,

Will come when it will come.

– Julius Caesar. William Shakespeare

Made in the USA